## "What are you trying to do to yourself?"

"I'm trying to get my life together again!" She threw the response back at him and his blue eyes flashed.

"Is that why you're wearing that boring dress, that shapeless jacket? And the body under them could be a boy's—you don't even look like a woman anymore! Your lovely hair has all been cut off. You aren't wearing makeup. You look terrible!"

"Leave me alone!" she broke out, resenting that description of herself. "It's my life, not yours. You don't have to live inside my head, so stay out of it. Please just go away and don't come back!"

D0967463

**CHARLOTTE LAMB** is one of Harlequin's best-loved and bestselling authors. Her extraordinary career has helped shape the face of romance fiction around the world.

Born in the East End of London, Charlotte spent her early childhood moving from relative to relative to escape the bombings of World War II. After working as a secretary in the BBC's European department, she married a political reporter who wrote for *The Times*. Charlotte recalls that it was at his suggestion that she began to write, "because it was one job I could do without having to leave our five children." Charlotte and her family now live in a beautiful home on the Isle of Man.

## Books by Charlotte Lamb

**HARLEQUIN PRESENTS PLUS**
1560—SLEEPING PARTNERS
1584—FORBIDDEN FRUIT
1672—FALLING IN LOVE

**HARLEQUIN PRESENTS**
1618—DREAMING
1658—FIRE IN THE BLOOD

# Charlotte Lamb

## Wounds of Passion

# Harlequin Books

TORONTO • NEW YORK • LONDON
AMSTERDAM • PARIS • SYDNEY • HAMBURG
STOCKHOLM • ATHENS • TOKYO • MILAN
MADRID • WARSAW • BUDAPEST • AUCKLAND

ISBN 0-373-11687-X

WOUNDS OF PASSION

# CHAPTER ONE

PATRICK OGILVIE flew into Nice Airport on a hot summer afternoon. As he headed towards the taxi ranks, walking fast, his tan leather suitcase in one hand, he heard someone calling his name.

'Patrick! Hey! Patrick!'

Stopping in mid-stride, startled, he turned and saw a girl hurrying towards him, looking more like a thin, graceful boy, in a black velvet jacket and sleek black jersey leggings, the only feminine thing about her outfit the jabot of white lace cascading down the front of her shirt.

'Rae! What the hell are you doing here?' Patrick was so taken aback that he couldn't even pretend to be pleased to see her, his brows heavy over his blue eyes; but Rae Dunhill didn't seem to notice; she flung her arms around him and hugged him.

'Graham rang early this morning and told me you were on this flight.' She was out of breath, laughing up at him. 'Thank heavens I spotted you; I was sure I was too late and had missed you. I got caught in a traffic jam on the motorway.'

'Our plane was delayed; we should have been here half an hour ago,' Patrick explained unsmilingly, his body rigid as he disengaged himself. 'You aren't staying in Nice too, are you? I thought you were somewhere on the Italian Riviera?'

'I am,' Rae nodded, and he caught the secret glance she gave him.

Patrick's frown deepened. He should never have told their joint editor, Graham Clive, that he was going to Nice, or at least not mentioned the time his plane left Heathrow. He might have known Graham would get in touch with Rae and tell her. What else had Graham told her?

'I'm staying at Bordighera, not far from the French border, with my American friends, Alex and Susan-Jane Holtner,' Rae told him. 'You remember Alex? He's the cartoonist. He does that very funny series about the American Indian in New York...you know, the one with the wigwam on top of a skyscraper.'

Patrick nodded indifferently. 'Oh, I know, yes, crazy sort of humour.'

'I love them,' Rae said indignantly. 'I was at school with Susan-Jane; she was my best friend. We've always kept in touch. She and Alex have a wonderful villa just outside Bordighera, on the coast road. They come every summer, for three months; they've been inviting me to stay for years, but I've always been too busy. This year, though, I finally managed to get some time off while they're here.'

'You certainly need a good break; you've been working hard for months,' Patrick said.

'So have you, Patrick. A few weeks in the sun is what you need, too,' said Rae, sliding her hand through his arm as they emerged into the hot sunshine of Nice. Patrick crinkled his eyes to peer at the ultra-blue sky, and, half blinded, slid dark glasses on to his nose.

'Yes, I am tired. That's why I'm here, to have a few weeks' peace and quiet.' He firmly pulled his arm free of her fingers, hoping she would get the message.

Rae wasn't that easy to discourage. 'You won't get that in a Nice hotel! You must come back to Bordighera with me—it was Alex's idea. He and Susan-Jane love to fill the villa with friends; they've been dying to meet you ever since I first mentioned you to them.'

Patrick's face set like concrete. 'No, thanks, very kind of them, but I've booked my hotel; I can't change the arrangement now.'

Rae fizzed with impatience. 'Of course you can! Don't be silly! And the villa is so comfortable—much nicer than some impersonal hotel. We can ring up and cancel your hotel room from the villa. It will only take us a few hours to get to Bordighera; the motorway's very fast.'

Typical, he thought grimly. There she goes again— trying to order me around! Ever since they'd started working together she had given him orders, rearranged his life, made decisions for him, as though she had some God-given right to do it, and he had never argued, because Rae Dunhill was someone he admired.

Only twenty-eight, she was already a best-selling writer. He had been a fan of her work long before he had met her and been invited to illustrate a new series of books she was working on.

Her children's books were extraordinary: original, sensitive, clever. Like Rae herself, he had to admit. She was fascinating—but she was also a woman of incredible energy and drive, who liked to run the lives of everyone around her, and Patrick didn't want to be managed by women any more, even for his own good.

'Very kind of your friends,' he curtly said, 'but I would rather go to my hotel. Sorry.' He didn't even try to look sorry, glowering into the blue distance of sea and sky. 'Look, Rae, I'm tired. I couldn't cope with having to make polite conversation with strangers.'

'I really think you should, Patrick,' Rae began, and he suddenly lost patience, and turned on her, with an angry snarl.

'Stop trying to run my life, will you?'

He felt her tense, staring. She had a memorable face, if not a beautiful one: thin, mobile, high-cheekboned, with brilliant dark eyes and thick, curly black hair cut short like a boy's, flicked back behind small, neat ears.

Carefully, she said, 'Sorry. Was I?'

'Yes, and please stop it; I can run my own life!'

Patrick turned away, shifted his case to another hand, and walked over towards the scrimmage which was what passed for a taxi queue outside the airport, hoping she would take the hint and go. She didn't, though; she followed him, watching him sideways. Patrick ignored her.

'Graham told me about Laura,' she softly said. 'I'm so sorry, Patrick.'

His profile tensed, dark colour invading his face. 'Graham talks too damn much!'

He had had lunch with Graham the day after his engagement was broken off; he couldn't think, talk, about anything but Laura. Graham was a good listener; he had made quiet, comforting noises, and Patrick had talked until he was hoarse. Now he wished to heaven he hadn't.

'I suppose you told your friends all about it, which is why I've been invited to their villa?' he bit out. 'Well, I don't need their sympathy—or yours, either, come to that. I'm not the first guy to get dumped by a woman, and I won't be the last! I won't die of it.'

'Of course you won't, and I didn't tell anyone else about Laura!' she said, her voice soothing; and that made him feel as edgy as a cat whose fur was being stroked the wrong way.

'I don't want to talk about her!' Patrick muttered. He couldn't bear to talk about Laura, and yet he couldn't stop thinking about her. How long did it take to get over this sort of pain? It wasn't like a headache, or even like a migraine—he had bad ones, sometimes, when he had been working very hard, whirring yellow lights and zigzags in front of his eyes turning him almost blind. At least you always knew they would be over within a matter of hours. You took a couple of pills and lay down in a darkened room to wait.

You couldn't do that with the sort of ache he had at the moment; there was no way of knowing how long it would last, and no pill you could take.

'It will take you ages to get a taxi in this mob,' Rae pointed out. 'At least let me drive you to your hotel.'

He hesitated, which, with Rae, was always fatal. 'Come on,' she coaxed, sliding her hand through his arm again, and he let her lead him across the road into the car park lined by palm trees.

As Rae unlocked her little red Fiat, he said roughly, 'But only if you promise not to ask any questions!'

'I won't even mention Laura,' Rae reassured, as they both got into the car.

But she had. Laura, he thought, the mere sound of the name opening a new wound in his heart. Oh, Laura, how could you do this to me?

When he was younger, he had never had a problem attracting girls—not that he was handsome; he had never been that. He had learnt in his teens, though, that he had *something*—he wasn't sure what it was, but he did know that for some reason girls liked him. Maybe it was his build—he had shot up when he was sixteen, to almost six feet, and he had a good body, because he liked sport, especially at school. He wasn't a beefy, hefty man, but he was wiry, his arms and legs tough and muscled, and he dressed well, kept his brown hair smoothly brushed.

But he had often thought it was his temperament girls went for—he was light-hearted, liked life on the sunny side, enjoyed being with other people, smiled a lot; and he hadn't taken anything seriously until he'd met Laura Grainger and fallen in love like Humpty Dumpty falling off a wall.

And now, like Humpty Dumpty, he was in pieces, and not all the King's horses or all the King's men could put him together again.

He had known from the start that Laura didn't love him as much as he loved her, and perhaps it was even her coolness that first attracted him? She was a challenge after years of finding it easy to get girls. One look at her, and Patrick had actually heard his heart beating. It had been an odd experience. That was how he'd known he was in love. What else could make you suddenly aware of your own heart beating? He'd never been aware of it before.

He had soon realised that Laura didn't just look cool—she was cool. She was beautiful and clever, quite accustomed to being chased by men; and very different from the other girls he had dated. They had been eager to wait on Patrick hand and foot—done his washing, cleaned his flat, cooked him meals. Laura hadn't; she was far too busy running her public relations agency. She wasn't the domesticated sort, either. They ate out quite often, and when they ate at home it was usually in Patrick's immaculate flat, and Patrick cooked the meal.

He had always enjoyed looking after himself; he was a practical man who was good at doing practical things.

Whether it was painting or modelling in clay or bronze, or ironing, cooking and cleaning, he was deft, with quick, capable hands; and he was intensely interested in detail. He had endless patience with objects, and people. Whatever the work, Patrick enjoyed the sense of satisfaction he got from a job well done, but it was even more of a pleasure to him when he was doing it for Laura.

Her name carried so many echoes, like remembered music—Laura, he thought; Laura, cool as a winter morning, distant as the dark blue horizon he saw as Rae's red Fiat turned into the Promenade des Anglais and sped along beside the sea.

He had always had a dream girl at the back of his mind, the sort of girl he wanted to marry one day, and the minute he had seen her he'd known Laura perfectly matched that image—with her cat-like green eyes and pale golden hair, the slender elegance of her body and that fine-boned face.

He'd once asked Laura, 'Did you ever daydream about the sort of man you wanted to marry?' Of course, he'd hoped she would tell him he was her dream come true.

'Of course, doesn't everybody?' she had smiled. 'I knew it would have to be a man who was ready to share everything with me—fifty-fifty. Who was cheerful about cooking supper if I was tired, or would do the shopping for me when I had to work late, who didn't expect me to wait on him the way my mother waited on my father, as if she were a servant and he were the lord and master. I made up my mind when I was very small that I'd never put up with that sort of relationship.'

How stupid could you be? he thought, his eyes dark. He had made himself everything he'd thought she wanted him to be; but she had still left him. Well, he'd never turn himself into a doormat for another woman. Doormats just got walked all over—the way Laura had walked all over him.

He had been a fool. He'd lied to himself, told himself she was too busy to have time for love; Laura was a high-powered and ambitious woman whose business drained all her energy and attention. Her emotions had been in deep freeze, but one day, he had believed, she would suddenly thaw, and he would be there.

He had been wildly wrong. Oh, she had suddenly thawed, but not for him—for another man.

For all Laura's talk about being a modern woman who would only marry a man who treated her like an equal, for all her claim to want a modern man who was ready to share the jobs around their home, who would happily change a nappy or do the ironing, who could be gentle, sympathetic, caring... for all that, she had ended up by dumping him for a man who was the exact opposite of everything she had said she wanted.

Patrick was still reeling from the shock. Who could have guessed? Oh, now and then he had worried that one day Laura might meet someone who really got to her in a way that Patrick knew he didn't. But never in a million years would he have suspected it could be Josh Kern.

The man Laura finally flipped over was an aggressive Yorkshire farmer who had put Laura's back up the minute she met him. It had never occurred to Patrick that she might actually find Josh Kern attractive. Laura was sophisticated and clever—what could she have in common with a farmer Patrick saw as some sort of Neanderthal, who rode over anyone who got in his way, who certainly showed no signs of being gentle or caring?

Patrick couldn't even imagine the guy changing a nappy, let alone cooking or doing the shopping.

From the first day she met Kern Laura had been very vocal on the subject of how much she disliked him, and Patrick had believed her until the other day, when he had arrived at her flat to find Kern there and to see the way they looked at each other. He had known in a flash, and hadn't needed to hear Laura admit she had fallen in love with the guy.

It showed in her eyes, in her face, even in her body. She had been alight with passion.

Patrick's jaw clenched. Rae caught sight of his tense face and instinctively put out a hand, touched his arm. 'Oh, Patrick, don't! I hate to see you so miserable!'

He jerked his arm away, scowling. 'Oh, for God's sake! How many times do I have to tell you? Leave me alone, can't you?'

Her kindness was like a fingertip laid on raw, burnt skin; the lightest brush was agony to him. He needed to be alone, to be quiet, to be still. Pain throbbed in his head, his veins, his heart. He wished to God Rae had not come to the airport.

'Which hotel?' Rae asked huskily a moment later, and when he told her, 'Oh, yes, I know it, one of the nineteenth-century hotels, lovely ironwork balconies,' she assured him, weaving in and out of the fast, busy traffic pouring along the Promenade des Anglais, the blue of the Baie des Anges on the right and the elegant façades of Nice hotels on the left.

'How's the new book coming?' Patrick asked curtly, and Rae accepted the change of subject, beginning to talk about her work.

She had written her first children's book when she was at university. A modern fairy-story, it was a runaway bestseller and was later made into a very successful film, with spin-offs from toys and games, making Rae Dunhill a very wealthy and famous writer.

Patrick had been very excited when she had asked him to illustrate the new series of books she was writing—international stories of mythology and legend. He'd leapt at the chance to work with a writer he admired, and he hadn't argued when Rae insisted he did everything her way.

Maybe that was my trouble! Patrick thought, his eyes moody. Maybe I was too eager to please; both her, and Laura. I never argued with either of them, let them ride roughshod over me. Did Laura come to despise me in the end? Stop thinking about her! he angrily told himself.

They left the Promenade, spun round a corner and then another; the sea breeze blew his brown hair across his face, and he raked it back with an impatient gesture, felt Rae giving him sideways glances, and sensed her trying to read his mind, which made his profile harden, resisting her.

'Here we are,' she said, pulling up outside his hotel.

'Thanks for the lift,' he said and managed a reluctant, apologetic smile. It wasn't Rae's fault that his engagement had been broken off, after all; and it had been very kind of her to drive all this way, across the Italian border, to come to the airport to meet him. He shouldn't have been so surly with her.

'I enjoyed the drive,' she assured him, then put a hand on his arm. 'Patrick...'

'Yes?' Not more questions! he thought, a little nerve twitching beside his mouth, while behind his sunglasses his blue eyes burnt fixedly on the bluer sky.

'Will you at least come over to Bordighera for the weekend? Alex gives famous barbecue parties on the beach; he's planning one for Saturday, and it will be terrific fun. Do come!'

'How many times do I have to tell you?' he broke out, then his voice shook and he had to stop speaking. He felt her watching his averted face and wanted to scream at her, Stop staring! Will you just leave me alone? But he couldn't; it would have been too much of a self-betrayal. He struggled to contain his rage, but felt as if his bones were pushing out through his tense skin. Then he caught sight of Rae's small hands trembling on the wheel, her knuckles showing white. There was a silence for a few minutes and Patrick stared out of the window without seeing anything.

Why am I taking it out on her? he thought. She's only a little thing, for all her bossiness and her self-assurance. It isn't her fault.

'OK,' he muttered. 'I'll come for Saturday night, but just for the weekend, Rae!'

'That's fine,' she said, breaking into a smile. 'I'm so glad, Patrick; I'm sure you'll have a great time, and you're going to love Alex and Susan-Jane. They've got a terrific sense of humour.'

'They'll need it, if they're to put up with me for a weekend,' Patrick said with bitter humour.

Rae laughed, then said hurriedly, her voice husky and unsure, stammering so that it didn't even sound like Rae talking, 'Patrick, I know you said you don't want to talk about it, but I have to ask...it wasn't...Laura wasn't...well, lately, I did wonder if...if she resented you being with me...being away so much, I mean? I remember she was upset when you had to change your plan to meet her in Amsterdam because I insisted we went back to Rome to do some more work there. That wasn't what you quarrelled over, was it? She wasn't...'

She broke off, very pink, then went on, 'She wasn't jealous over me, was she, Patrick? I'd hate to think I'd been the cause of you two breaking up.'

Patrick gave a curt bark of angry amusement. 'Odd you should say that. Laura did make some stupid remark about you and me, hinting that I might be interested in you.'

Rae's face turned scarlet. 'Oh, no...'

'There's no need to look like that—that wasn't why we split up! She was just using you as an excuse, and I told her she needn't try to pretend she believed anything so crazy!'

Rae's hot colour drained away, leaving her pale. 'Yes, of course—it would be crazy,' she said flatly.

Patrick was scowling up at the elegant white façade of the hotel, built during the Second Empire, with that faint trace of fantasy, of over-decoration.

'She couldn't possibly have believed it; she was only trying to use you as an excuse,' he said grimly. 'She wouldn't have to feel guilty if she could kid herself I was interested in another woman.'

'She must be out of her mind, preferring someone else to you!' Rae broke out, and he laughed harshly.

'I won't argue with that!'

Rae watched him anxiously. 'Patrick, I'm so——'

'Don't say sorry again!' he snarled, and she flinched as if he had hit her.

The blare of a horn made them both look at the road. Nice was a parking nightmare, too many cars looking for too few parking spaces, and sometimes people double-parked, even triple-parked if they dared.

Rae's car was blocking the narrow road, which was already crammed with parked cars. Another car wanted to get past—it was wider, and the driver was incensed.

Rae hurriedly dragged on the wheel, moving up on to the pavement to let the other car pass. The driver leaned over to bellow something very rude in French as he shot through, and Rae made apologetic gestures at him. Being a Frenchman, he mellowed enough to give her a forgiving wave and a shake of his head; she was, after all, chic and very female.

'I'd better get out, before you get fined for parking on the pavement!' Patrick said, opening the car door.

'I'll come and pick you up here, on Saturday morning, OK?' Rae said as he collected his suitcase from the car. 'Ten o'clock sharp? Then we can get to the villa in time for lunch. Make sure you have your passport.'

Patrick nodded and ran into the hotel. Minutes later he was in his room, which had a sideways view of the Baie des Anges through palm trees. He undressed and took a long, cooling shower, lay down on his bed wearing only a towel, and went to sleep with the shutters of his room closed, excluding the hot afternoon sun.

He had decided to go to the Côte d'Azur because it was not a place he knew well, and he had hoped he wouldn't run into anyone he knew. He was still trying to make sense of what had happened to him, but it was hard when he felt as if he had broken into pieces—little jagged, dagger-sharp pieces that hurt like hell whenever he tried to touch them or explore the damage that had been done to him.

All he knew so far was that nothing in his life would ever be the same again, especially himself, and that he needed to be alone for a long time, to come to terms with what had happened to him.

He ate dinner in a little restaurant near his hotel, which, like many small French hotels, did not have a restaurant, went for a stroll in white jeans and a thin

T-shirt, sat at a terrace bar drinking a beer, then went to bed listening to the constant hum of Nice traffic.

In the morning he got up, ate croissants, drank coffee, went for a walk down to the beach, and sunbathed until lunchtime. He ate lunch on the beach at a busy restaurant—a salad niçoise and French bread, a glass or two of white wine, a coffee. Then he went back to his room and closed the shutters and took a shower and went to sleep on his bed again, got up as evening began, ate dinner at the same restaurant, went for a stroll to the same bar, drank a beer, went to bed.

The days passed in a dull routine which soothed the anger and the pain in him by sheer monotony, and then it was Saturday and Rae arrived, as she had promised, her short black hair windblown after her drive across the border, her eyes bright, her smile warm. She was wearing a light summer dress in white cotton printed with violets and soft green leaves.

She gave him a wary look which tried to assess his mood. 'Ready?'

He had bought himself a new overnight bag, which he had packed with a few things. He threw them into the back of her car, nodding, climbed in beside her, and they set off. In a short time they were on the toll road, heading along the coast, towards the Italian border. Rae drove with skill and daring, talking all the time about her ideas for the illustrations to the next set of stories.

They arrived at the border and queued up for nearly half an hour before they got through.

'The border is always busy on a Saturday. Weekends are the worst times to cross,' Rae said, then asked casually, 'What are you going to do when we've finished the work on the books? Will you go back to York to live?'

He shook his head without looking at her. He wanted to be a thousand miles away from anything that could remind him of Laura. If he returned to the city where he had lived for years he would be bound to run into her all the time.

'What will you do, then?' Rae persevered.

'I thought I might settle in Italy.'

He felt Rae's leap of surprise, caught the quick sideways look she gave him. She hadn't expected that. Well, good. He meant to be unpredictable and unexpected in future; he might as well start now.

They were waved through the border a few minutes later and drove along the *autostrada* to Bordighera, then turned down the hill from the old town towards the sea. Slowing, Rae leaned out of the car and tapped a security number into a panel beside a high metal gate, operated electronically. The gates swung open and they drove through, down a winding path between cypress trees, olive trees and bougainvillaea.

Patrick stared up at the villa they were approaching; it was enormous, built on a number of levels, a confusion of white walls, red-tiled roofs, dark window-frames and black-painted shutters. A fir tree grew close to the house, dropping pine cones on the paving-stones; geraniums tumbled out of pots, a tortoiseshell cat slept on a stone seat by the front door, and roses and lavender filled the air with fragrance; it was a lovely place.

'Isn't it magic?' asked Rae, observing his reaction with pleasure.

Alex and Susan-Jane Holtner came out to meet them as they parked outside the villa.

'Hi, there, welcome,' Alex said, shaking hands warmly, smiling. He was a very tall, thin man of over forty, with reddish hair, a thin moustache, dark glasses and freckles.

'Hallo. I'm Patrick Ogilvie—it's very good of you to invite me,' said Patrick, trying not to stare at the man's wife too much. It wasn't easy; she was stunning, in one of the tiniest bikinis he had ever seen.

Tall, sexy, with a ravishing model figure, she was years younger than her husband. Her rich chestnut hair framed her face in a wild tangle of curls, and she had wide blue eyes, a classical nose and a full, generous mouth.

'Susan-Jane, my wife,' said Alex Holtner, a gleam of humour in his eye, and Patrick shook hands with her, struggling not to look down at the warm ripeness of the body spilling out of the bikini.

'Rae never stops talking about what a genius you are; we have been aching to meet you,' she said, then, mischievously, 'Alex is quite jealous of you!'

'I wish I could paint half as well, but all I can do is draw cartoons,' her husband said complacently, sliding an arm around her and patting her on the bottom.

'Brilliant cartoons,' Patrick said, smiling. 'I've followed them ever since they started appearing.'

Alex grinned at him. 'Why, thank you. Now the compliments are over, Rae will show you your room. If there's anything you need, just ask. Oh, and we were going to eat lunch on the terrace—just salad and bread. Is that OK with you, Patrick?'

'Sounds wonderful to me; it's much too hot to eat much down here, I find,' Patrick said.

'And the wine makes you sleepy,' said Susan-Jane.

'But it's such a good excuse for going to bed in the afternoon,' her husband said wickedly, grinning down at her, and she gave him a little punch.

'Don't be naughty!'

Patrick felt a stab of pain at the intimacy between them; that was something else he was going to miss.

The party began before it grew dark that evening; people began arriving in cars or on foot from nearby villas, flocking into the villa gardens which tumbled down to the beach. The barbecue site was just above the beach, and close to the enormous blue-tiled swimming-pool set into a wide terrace, where they could set out chairs and tables around a bar counter from which drinks could be served. Earlier, Patrick had helped carry chairs, knives and forks, trays of glasses and plates down to the terrace, and watched Alex testing the lighting, setting up the music system.

Now there were brightly coloured lights strung through the trees and pop music floated out into the darkening sky. Some guests were swimming in the pool, a few were dancing, some wandered under the trees, and others sat by the bar and talked.

Patrick wandered between the various groups, took a glass of red wine, sipped it as he walked, paused to watch a girl swimming in the pool, strolled on to stare at the dancers, and felt his heart turn over violently as he caught sight of long, pale gold hair, a slender body in a silky white dress which ended at the thighs, and below that, long, elegant legs.

For a moment he thought it really was Laura. He took three hurried steps towards her, barely breathing.

Then the music stopped and the girl and her partner broke apart; she turned and Patrick hungrily stared, but her face was nothing like Laura's. The thick beating of his heart slowed; he felt a burst of rage, as if the girl had deliberately deceived him.

She was staring straight at him now, as if she had picked up his intense concentration on her, half smiling.

Her eyes were blue, not green, he noted dully. She was young, not more than twenty, her face heart-shaped, with a softness in the curve of the cheek and jawline, a fullness in the mouth, that was completely different from the delicacy of Laura's features.

He turned away, heart-sick, finished his red wine, and put the glass down.

'Come and dance!' said a voice beside him, and he swung round, stiffening.

He knew it was her before he saw her; she had a light, young voice with a distinct accent. American, he thought. Some relative of Alex Holtner? He remembered over lunch some talk of a niece, a young art student, coming down that day for the party from Florence, where she was spending the summer studying Renaissance art. He had barely listened, indifferent to everything they said.

'You do speak English?' she asked, watching him secretly, her eyes half veiled by long, curling lashes loaded with mascara; shyness mingled with silent invitation in the way the full mouth curved in a smile.

The neckline of the silk dress was low; you could see a lot of golden tanned flesh, the cleft between her small, high breasts.

She moved closer, put out a hand to him; and he was tempted for a moment. He could pretend, just for a little while, hold that slender body in his arms, touch her and pretend she was Laura. It would be so easy.

Her fingers brushed slowly along his bare arm, sending a wave of self-disgust through him.

'I don't dance, thanks,' he said brusquely, and turned and walked away. It would have been madness, like an alcoholic taking just one more drink, kidding himself it wouldn't be a risk. He would never forget Laura that way, and it would have been unforgivable to use that girl as a puppet in his private fantasies. She was so young, skin like a peach, tiny fair hairs giving her that shimmer, that radiance; and she had had an unconscious sensuality in the swing of her hips, in the rich curve of her mouth.

She had aroused him with her faint resemblance to the woman he loved. He was too restless now to stay around at the party. He walked out of the glare of lights, away from the blare of the music, the laughter and voices, into the shadows of the trees, down through the gardens to the beach, took off his sandals and walked barefoot through the creaming surf. He headed off along the beach with no real idea of where he was going, sat down on the sand to stare out over the sea for half an hour or so, then got up, brushed the sand off his jeans, and walked back up through the gardens to the villa.

Everyone seemed to be down around the pool, eating and drinking; he skirted the lights and managed to slip into the house without running into anyone, went to his room, took off his clothes, dropped them on a chair, and got into bed, naked, because it was so hot.

Outside the party was in full swing, noisier than ever; but Patrick's shutters were closed and he was so exhausted, emotionally and physically, that he drifted off to sleep.

He woke up some time later when the door burst open with a crash and men poured into the room.

Dazed, blinking, as the room light was switched on, Patrick sat up in the bed, a sheet falling off his smooth brown shoulders.

'What the devil do you think you're doing?'

The intruders fanned out around the room, watching him as if expecting him to do something violent. They were wearing uniform. His mind, still half asleep, registered: wasn't that Carabinieri uniform? Policemen? he thought blankly; what on earth was going on? Had somebody burgled the villa while the party was going on, while he slept?

'Patrick Ogilvie?'

Patrick's head jerked round towards the man who had spoken in English, a short, broad man in his forties, black-haired, pugnacious-looking, who needed a shave, his olive skin rough around the jaw.

'Yes, I'm Patrick Ogilvie. Who are you? What is all this? What are you doing, bursting into my room like this in the middle of the night?'

'I am Brigadier Saltini of the Carabinieri. Please get dressed; I cannot interview you while you are naked in bed—do you always sleep naked?' The man's black eyes focused on Patrick's clothes, thrown across the back of the chair. 'Is that what you wore last night? What are those stains on the jeans? Salt water? Sand? You went down to the beach, then?' He jerked his head, and one of the other men produced a plastic bag, put on transparent white plastic gloves, and began carefully sliding Patrick's clothes into the bag.

'Why is he doing that? Why are you taking my clothes away? What's going on?' Patrick was feeling chilled, distinctly disturbed now. He didn't like the way these policemen watched him; there was a coldness in their eyes.

Calmly, Brigadier Saltini said, 'How long have you been in bed, Mr Ogilvie?'

'I don't know—I've been asleep.' Patrick looked at the time shown on his watch, which he had left on the bedside table overnight. 'Two hours, maybe?'

'Are you sure? You didn't come to bed just around an hour ago?'

'No, longer than that.'

'Well, will you get up and get dressed, and come down to the station house, please?' the brigadier asked him.

'Not until I know what this is all about, and not in front of all these people!' Patrick said stubbornly.

The brigadier nodded his head towards the door, and the other men filtered out.

'A girl has been attacked,' the brigadier said quietly, and Patrick looked at him in shock and disbelief.

'Rae? Not Rae?'

The brigadier slowly shook his head, and watched him, frowning, as Patrick relaxed again on an unconscious sigh of relief.

'That was not her name, *Signore*. She was a guest at this party—an American girl, with blonde hair. You spoke to her, I think. Do you remember talking to her?'

Patrick sat very still. 'Yes,' he whispered, sickened. 'That girl?'

'You were seen watching her,' said the brigadier. 'Staring fixedly at her, some witnesses said.'

'She looked like . . . like someone I know . . . knew.'

Patrick pushed aside memories of Laura, thought of the other girl: her shy, half-veiled eyes, her young, golden skin, the beauty of her slim body, her instinctive, innocent sensuality.

'She was so young,' he said, to himself. 'Barely out of her teens.' Then he was struck by a new idea and looked sharply at the other man. 'I hardly even spoke to her! Why do you need to talk to me?'

The brigadier's hard black eyes watched him closely. 'Her description of the man fits you exactly.'

# CHAPTER TWO

TWO years later, Patrick was still having nightmares about what had happened to him over the hours that followed. Not every night, just whenever he was tense over something, worried, upset. On a night like that he would find himself back there, in that time, dreaming it over and over again, in slow, terrifying sequence.

The brigadier had left one of his younger officers in the room to watch him dress, and Patrick had instinctively hurried, putting on the first clothes that came to hand—clean underwear, clean jeans, a crisp blue T-shirt, socks, and another pair of trainers since the police had removed the sandals he had been wearing last night. He had needed to go to the lavatory urgently, been allowed to do so after the brigadier was consulted, had washed his hands and face and combed his hair, but he had had to leave the bathroom door open, and the officer had stood outside and watched him out of the corner of an eye.

'Do you have to stand there?' Patrick had burst out, and the man had nodded.

'Orders, my orders,' he said in thick English.

All that had been mere pinpricks; yet already Patrick felt uneasy, off balance; he was sweating, and yet he didn't know why.

He knew he was innocent, after all. He hadn't done anything to that girl. Yet his stomach was queasy, he felt his nerves jumping, and his mouth was dry. And his head buzzed with questions.

Why had she given them his description? What was going to happen now? Where were they taking him? What ought he to do?

'OK, let's go!' the young officer said, grabbing his arm as he came out of the bathroom, pushing him towards the stairs. As Patrick stumbled he thought he heard the other man mutter, '*Mi dispiace molto per lei!*' and only later understood what the officer had said— I'm sorry for you!

Patrick wasn't sure what he had meant and couldn't ask, but it had not been a friendly remark. It wasn't pity or compassion he meant; there was hostility, distaste, in the young man's eyes. It had been a veiled threat, meaning Patrick was going to be sorry for himself.

Self-pity wasn't what Patrick was feeling, though. He was worried, he was frightened, but most of all he was angry; blazingly angry.

He hadn't done anything—so why was this happening to him?

As he was hustled through the villa they passsed one of the main rooms of the house, a huge marble-floored lounge hung with cartoons, modern paintings and mirrors, where Patrick had sat earlier, talking to Rae before the party began, drinking chilled white wine.

It was full of people now—the guests from the party, he imagined—all seated, none of them talking. Faces turned towards the door; he recognised some of them, couldn't put names to them. They stared at him, and he felt himself go dark red, in spite of knowing he was not guilty. Their eyes made him feel guilty.

That was when he realised they believed he was guilty—and the cold sweat sprang out on his forehead.

Alex Holtner was there, a jacket round his shoulders as if he was cold, sitting on a stool, looking pale and haggard. He stared across the room, and his eyes were full of loathing. He glared, clenched his fists on his knees as if longing to hit Patrick, then half rose as if to cross the room to get him. Susan-Jane Holtner was curled up on the floor next to her husband, leaning on him; she put her hands over Alex's, whispering something, and Alex looked down at her, subsiding again.

A second later Patrick was past, being rushed towards the open front door. It was night, yet the front of the villa was ablaze with light. The police had set up flood-lights; there were police cars parked everywhere; police-men moved to and fro, absorbed in whatever they were doing. But they all looked round as Patrick came out of the front door, froze, staring. He was pushed into the back of a police car just as another drove away, past him; and with a pang of shock he saw Rae in it. Her face was chalk-white, her eyes like bruises in her skin. She saw him at the last moment, turned her head to stare back, her pale lips parting, her eyes urgent, as if trying to say something to him.

Did she, too, believe he was guilty?

She knew him, for God's sake! Patrick thought. She couldn't possibly believe he would do something like this, surely? Surely.

He wished he could have talked to her, told her... But would she believe him? She looked so shocked. He felt sick. If even Rae believed he had done it! He was almost coming to believe he had, himself! It was the way people looked at you, the waves of hatred coming from them.

Years later, dreaming about it, he had the same dis-orientating impression of being trapped in a living nightmare; he kept hoping he was asleep and dreaming, that this couldn't really be happening to him.

The difference was, years later, that he did wake up.

At the time, there was no escape for him. He had to go where they took him, helpless in their hands.

As the car drove out of the villa the policeman sitting in the back with him grabbed the back of his neck with one large hand, pushed his head down, and held it there. 'Paparazzi!' he grunted in explanation, and Patrick was feeling so dazed that for a moment he didn't get the point.

Then, as the car slowed to turn out into the road, he heard an outburst of noise: people pressing around the sides of the car, pushing and rocking it, hands banging on the windows. Flash bulbs went off, the car was full of brightness exploding like lightning, people shouted and yelled; then the car shot forward at great speed and he was thrown forward too, and hit his head with a thud on the back of the seat in front. The policeman beside him hauled him up by the slack of his shirt, almost tearing it. Patrick felt dizzy, and his forehead hurt, throbbed. He would have a bruise there tomorrow.

The drive was a short one, and he was forced to go through the same humiliating procedure of crouching down out of sight as the car shot into the police car park, then the officers put a blanket over his head and ran him into the building.

The first person he saw was a man in a white coat who seemed to be a doctor. He told Patrick to strip again, then gave him a medical examination in great detail. To Patrick it felt as if the man was crawling over his body with a microscope; every orifice was examined, every pore in his skin, every hair on his head, it seemed. Samples of his blood, urine, even his perspiration, were taken.

Swabs were taken, too, from under his nails, in his mouth, and other places, while Patrick suffered it, white-faced and dark-eyed with humiliation.

By the time he reached the brigadier's office he was even angrier, and he was thinking coherently again. The first shock had worn off; he was fighting back.

'I want a lawyer,' he said as soon as he saw the senior officer again. 'I'm entitled to a lawyer; you can't refuse to let me see one—an English-speaking one—and I think I'd better speak to the British consul first and ask his advice on who should represent me.'

'All in good time. It's your right, of course, but this is only a preliminary interview—we aren't charging you yet—so first we have to establish that you are going to need a lawyer, surely?' The black eyes were shrewd, watchful, hard. 'Or are you admitting your guilt?'

'No!' The word exploded. Patrick paused, flushed and tense. 'No,' he said more calmly. 'I haven't done any-thing to be guilty about.'

'Well, then, no need for lawyers and consuls,' smiled the brigadier bluffly, and Patrick almost began to feel easier, then the man added, 'Yet!' and the fear kick-started into life again.

'Sit down, Mr Ogilvie,' the brigadier said. 'I am going to have some coffee—would you like some?'

Patrick nodded.

'Black? Milk? Sugar?'

'Black, sugar,' Patrick said, and the brigadier lifted a phone, gave an order, leaned back in his chair, and tapped a pencil on the desk in front of him.

'This interview is being recorded . . .' he began. 'Those present are . . .'

There were two other men, as well as the brigadier, one in uniform, one in civilian clothes. Their names were given; Patrick didn't ever consciously remember them later. He remembered their faces, most of all their eyes, watching him.

Patrick was to spend hours in that room that night, endlessly going over the same ground. The brigadier was a thorough man, patient and obsessed with detail.

He kept coming back to Patrick's behaviour at the barbecue, asking him why he had stared at the blonde girl.

'It was noticed, the way you couldn't take your eyes off her. We have lots of witnesses.' He picked up a pile of typed pages; the leaves of paper fluttered as his fingers riffled them.

'All these people saw you staring fixedly at her. Why were you staring, Mr Ogilvie?'

It was the one point on which Patrick felt any guilt. He was uneasy every time they went back to that. Half sullenly, he muttered, 'I told you—she reminded me of someone.'

'Who?'

Patrick's upper lip was sweating. 'A girl I know.'

The brigadier watched him relentlessly. 'Miss Laura Grainger?'

It was like cold water in the face. Patrick sat still, white. 'I never told you her name. Who told you...?' Rae, he thought; Rae told him. Did Rae see me staring at that girl? Did Rae pick up that haunting similarity, the shifting, fragmentary likeness to Laura which had deceived him for a moment? One minute it had been there, the next it had gone, dissolving like a reflection when a hand broke the still surface of the water, yet leaving ripples and broken particles where it had been.

What had Rae thought when she saw him staring at the girl? What had she thought when she heard the girl had been attacked, that the girl had given Patrick's description to the police?

Was that why she had told them about Laura? Did Rae think he was guilty, that he had attacked that girl because she reminded him of Laura?

And that was the core of his uneasiness: that in his mind now he was confusing her with Laura. He had to keep reminding himself that it wasn't Laura who had been attacked, but some other girl, a stranger, someone he didn't even know.

He tried to stop muddling them up like that, but as the night wore on and he got more and more tired he kept forgetting. His mind blurred their images; they merged inside in his head—pale, slender girls with long gold hair and lovely bodies. They danced in his mind like candle-flames; dazzling and blinding him, making it even harder to think clearly, to keep his attention on the questions being asked.

'You were very distressed by the ending of your engagement to Miss Grainger,' the brigadier softly insinuated. 'Angry and humiliated. Any man would be—to lose his woman to another man! You must have wanted to kill them both.'

His face tightened, white and bitter. He had. Of course he had. Not Laura! he thought quickly; he would never have hurt Laura. But Kern. He could kill him, and feel no flicker of regret.

'And then at this party you saw a girl who reminded you of the woman you loved, the woman who had betrayed you, rejected you. How did you feel, Mr Ogilvie? What were you thinking as you stood there staring at her so fixedly?'

He had thought it was Laura; for one crazy, terrible second he had thought she had followed him to Italy, had come to say she had changed her mind, that she had realised she loved him, not Kern, after all.

All that had gone through his head in a flash as he stood there staring, and then she had turned and he had realised his mistake. He had fallen from a great height at that moment: all the way from heaven to hell.

He stared at the brigadier, not really seeing him.

'You had a strange expression on your face, some witnesses say,' the policeman said, flicking through the reports again, without taking his eyes off Patrick. 'You turned away, and then the girl walked over to you—what did she say to you, Mr Ogilvie?'

'She asked if I wanted to dance,' Patrick absently said, had already told him a hundred times. Sometimes Patrick almost invented something new to say, simply to break the monotony; but he wasn't crazy enough, yet, not stupid enough, yet. Once he did that he was lost.

'Is that all she said?'

Patrick's temper snapped again; his mouth writhed in a sneer. 'Surely your observant witnesses have told you that!'

The brigadier gazed stolidly at him. 'If you would bear with me, Mr Ogilvie. I have to be certain about details. So, Miss Cabot came over to you——'

'Cabot?' It was the first time the girl's name had been mentioned; Patrick couldn't help the startled question.

The brigadier waited, watching with the patience of a fisherman who thought he might have got a bite on his line.

'That's her name?' Patrick asked.

'Antonia Cabot,' the brigadier told him, and there was a strange echo inside Patrick's head, as if he had heard the name before; and maybe he had, from Rae, or the

Holtners, when they had spoken about Alex's niece, the art student, coming from Florence.

'Antonia Cabot,' he said huskily, aloud, and shivered. It was a beautiful name and she was lovely—what had happened to her last night?

The brigadier watched him shiver, his eyes narrowing.

'A beautiful girl,' he said softly. 'Young, blonde, desirable...'

Patrick thought of her as he had first seen her, dancing with another man, her body moving sensually, lightly, with gaiety.

She had come over to him, smiled at him, with that shy, unconscious invitation; and he had been bitterly angry because she looked so much like Laura, but wasn't Laura, and because...

He swallowed, feeling sick, perspiration on his face.

'You wanted her,' the brigadier said, and the words echoed what he had almost thought just now, what he wished he could pretend he had never thought.

He almost screamed, Yes! because it was true, although he wished it weren't. Yes, he had wanted her. He had looked at that lovely face, that lovely body, and wanted her, but she wasn't Laura, and he wasn't interested in a one-night stand with some unknown girl just because she looked like Laura, so he had turned his back and walked away.

Why had she told the police that the man who had attacked her looked like him?

Or was him? Had she actually said it was him? Why would she say that? Had she lied? Or simply been confused? The questions ran round and round inside his head.

'Why won't you tell me exactly what happened?' he broke out. 'You keep asking me questions, but you never answer mine. Was the girl attacked at the party? In the gardens? In the house? Didn't anybody see, hear, anything? There were all those people around; surely somebody must have seen something?'

'They saw you, Mr Ogilvie,' the brigadier said, 'walking down through the gardens, to the beach. They saw you. She saw you go, too, the girl, Antonia Cabot. She was sorry for you. She thought you looked unhappy, and her uncle later told her about your broken engagement. So she followed you, down to the beach, with some idea, I suppose, of talking to you, comforting you. She saw the trail of your footsteps along the sand and followed them, fitting her own feet into them, she said; it was some sort of game, I gathered.' The brigadier looked faintly indulgent. 'She is very young. And then suddenly someone jumped out at her from behind a boat; she caught a brief impression by moonlight of a face, light brown hair, a T-shirt, jeans. She thought it was you, playing a trick on her; she began to laugh.'

'It wasn't me; I never saw her on the beach!' Patrick said.

The brigadier just watched him, then went on, 'Then something hit her on the head, and she lost consciousness. She doesn't know how long she was out, but when she came round she had been gagged with sticky tape; she couldn't scream, and her attacker had taped her eyes, too, so she couldn't see him, but he spoke to her, she said. In English; it was an English accent. She said it sounded like your voice.'

'I only spoke to her once; I said one sentence to her! How could she possibly know what I sound like from that?'

'You were on the beach, Mr Ogilvie?'

'Yes, but——'

'Your clothes were covered in sand and salt water.'

'I sat down on the sand for a long time, but I didn't see that girl, and I did not attack her!'

'Tell me again why you went down to the beach, Mr Ogilvie,' the brigadier began again, and Patrick felt as if his head was going to explode.

'I'm tired; I need sleep,' he said wearily. 'You can't keep me here all this time without letting me see a lawyer. I insist you let me make a phone call to the British consul.'

'We have telephoned a lawyer on your behalf and he will be coming to see you quite soon,' the brigadier promised. 'And the British consul will see you in the morning. After the identity parade.'

Patrick froze. 'Identity parade?'

'Miss Cabot is in hospital tonight, but I'm told she is prepared to see if she can identify you in a line-up tomorrow. She is a very brave girl.'

Patrick saw an Italian lawyer, small, thin, dark, and red-eyed from being woken up in the middle of the night, who had a thick summer cold, which made him sneeze constantly and depressed him.

'The girl's evidence is bad news, Signor Ogilvie. She identifies you almost certainly, by sight, and by sound, places you on the spot at that time, as do a number of other witnesses, and you yourself admit you were there on the beach at that time. Nobody else from the party was down there on that part of the beach. They all have alibis; they were all with other people at the relevant time. And you had recently broken up with your fiancée, which makes the police feel they can prove motive as well as opportunity.'

'I didn't do it!' Patrick hoarsely said.

'Of course,' the lawyer said, smiling indifferently. 'They haven't yet got the forensic results—the various tests on you and the girl. They will come in tomorrow or the next day. The problem is...the attacker was scared off before he actually raped the girl; apparently he heard voices, people coming towards them, and ran off, and then the girl ripped off the tape on her mouth and eyes, and crawled into the sea——'

'Why on earth did she do that?'

The lawyer looked coolly at him. 'Common behaviour pattern in these cases. She felt dirty; she wanted to wash herself clean; the sea was the nearest place. She says she swam for some time. She may have been feeling suicidal, of course. The police didn't mention that, but I'd say it was on her mind.'

Patrick leaned forward, feeling sick, dropping his head into his hands. 'And I thought I had problems,' he muttered. 'God, what a mess.'

His lawyer said quietly, 'Unfortunately, she practically wiped out most of the forensic evidence—which would be good, if you were guilty, because it would mean they couldn't prove it, but as it is our case that you are innocent it makes our job harder as we can't prove you didn't!'

'Are you saying it's hopeless?' asked Patrick, and the lawyer shook his head.

'Of course not. No, but let's hope she doesn't pick you out at the identity parade.'

'She will,' Patrick said with grim certainty.

'Be careful—that sounds like a confession,' his lawyer quickly said.

'I can't help what it sounds like—I can only keep telling you, I didn't do it. But she thinks I did. I told you what happened at the party. I wouldn't dance with her; I turned my back on her and walked away. She'll pick me out.'

The lawyer looked shocked. 'Are you saying that she lied to the police? That she knows it was not you, but has accused you of it, deliberately, just because you wouldn't dance with her? I find that very hard to believe, Mr Ogilvie, and so will the police.'

'Women do unbelievable things,' said Patrick bitterly. 'You can't trust them or rely on them. She'll pick me out, you'll see.'

She did.

Patrick stood in a line of other men of roughly his build and height and colouring, staring straight ahead. First of all, the girl must have looked at them through a two-way mirror on the wall opposite—then after a few moments some policemen and two policewomen came out of a door, and she was with them, walking slowly, unsteadily.

Partrick kept his eyes ahead, as he had been ordered to do; she walked along the line and looked at the men one by one. Patrick's heart began to beat hard and thickly as she came nearer, then she was in front of him and he looked straight at her.

She was deathly pale, her gold hair tied back starkly from her face, dark glasses on her nose, hiding her eyes. But he saw the evidence of what had been done to her, and his stomach clenched in sickness. There were bruises like blue stains on her cheekbones, under her eyes, around her puffy, discoloured lips, and bite-marks on her neck above the high-collared cotton sweater she wore.

There was a heavy silence; the policemen all looked at Patrick. She looked at him, too, her eyes hidden by the dark glass shielding them.

Then she put out a hand that shook visibly, almost touched his shoulder, then turned away so fast that she almost fell over. A policewoman put an arm around her and helped her out, her body limp and trembling.

'I didn't do it!' Patrick called out after her; but he was grabbed, hustled back to the cells, and locked in until the brigadier was ready to talk to him again.

Patrick spent another day in custody, of relentless questioning, while they waited for the forensic evidence to be analysed. Halfway through the long, long evening, when his eyes were drooping and he was shaking with exhaustion, the brigadier was called out to take a phone call.

He came back looking shaken. He stood in front of Patrick, staring at him, very pale, while Patrick, even paler with nervous dread by then, stared back at him.

'What?' he broke out. 'What's happened now?'

The brigadier took a deep breath and said rather stiffly, 'Mr Ogilvie, it is my duty to offer you a most sincere apology on behalf of myself and this company of Carabinieri. We accept your innocence of the charge, and you are entirely free to leave.'

Patrick was so tired that for a minute he didn't understand. 'What are you talking about?'

'You are free to go, Mr Ogilvie,' repeated the brigadier. 'The man who attacked Miss Cabot is in custody in San Remo—he raped another girl, there, last night, and was caught, and, during interrogation, confessed to having tried to rape Miss Cabot. When his hotel room was searched certain objects were found, which had been taken from Miss Cabot during the attack; a ring and some underwear. There is no doubt—he was the man.'

Patrick sat as if turned to stone. 'Was he English?'

The brigadier nodded. 'I gather he does have a super-ficial resemblance to you, too. The same colouring, build, height. That must have been what deceived Miss Cabot into believing it was you.'

Patrick did not believe that. She had described him to the police because she had resented the way he walked away from her after she asked him to dance. Oh, it might have been an unconscious response; but Patrick did not believe it was pure coincidence.

'We will be happy to drive you back to the villa in a police car, right away,' the brigadier said.

Patrick shook his head. 'Am I free to leave Italy? I would rather return to my hotel in Nice immediately, if that is OK with you. I don't want to go back to the Holtner villa. Could my belongings left there be sent on to me? Could you arrange that? I don't want to see any of those people again. If you need my evidence later, of course, I'll come back, any time.'

The brigadier was eager to co-operate, to do as he wished. A car took Patrick over the border that night, back to his hotel in Nice. He stayed there a few more days, mostly alone in his room, lying on his bed, sleeping and waking, obsessed with the events of those days and nights.

They never did call him to give evidence; Patrick read about the case later, in the Italian papers, and dis-covered that the arrested man had been convicted of a series of rapes along that coast that summer. Antonia Cabot's name was only one among many and she had not even been called to give evidence.

Rae came to see Patrick in Nice a few days later. She had rung first, found him out, and left a message to say she was coming. He was waiting.

They went for a walk through the narrow, labyrinthine streets of the old town, with its medieval houses and street markets, crumbling plaster on walls, geraniums tumbling down from pots on balconies and ancient shutters with cracked and blistered paint, and made their way up alleys and through tiny cobbled squares.

'I don't know what to say; it's been terrible. It must have been a nightmare for you,' Rae told him, giving him uncertain, nervous sideways looks.

'Yes,' said Patrick grimly, unsmiling.

'They questioned me about you for hours,' Rae said.

He had guessed that, guessed where the brigadier was getting all his inside information from, who was giving them clues about his mental condition, his possible motive for attacking a woman. There was only one person who knew all about Laura, all about Patrick's moods since his engagement was broken off.

Rae stared at his hard profile, burst out, 'Oh, Patrick, I'm sorry. I feel so badly about this. I never thought you did it; I know you better than that! But...but...they seemed so sure; they said she had identified you, and you were in such a strange mood, you were angry over Laura, you were upset—I didn't know what to think.'

He stopped, his hands driven deep into the pockets of a black linen jacket he was wearing over black jeans, and stared broodingly over the steep streets of old Nice falling away below them.

'What do you want me to say, Rae? That I understand? That I forgive you for believing I could have tried to rape a young girl?'

'I didn't believe it, Patrick!'

He turned and looked at her directly, his face bleak. 'Oh, yes, you did, Rae. I saw your face when they were driving you away. That girl identified me, God knows why. You believed her, although you've known me pretty well for a long time, and you fed the police with the sort of evidence they needed to convince them I had a motive, too. If it wasn't for sheer damned luck I might be waiting trial now, on that charge, with very little hope of getting off. So if you're expecting me to say I forgive you and it doesn't matter that you believed I was a vicious rapist, I'm afraid you're out of luck.'

She bit her lip, very pale. 'Of course I know how you must feel——'

'I doubt it! A month ago I would have described myself as a very happy man—I was about to marry the woman I loved, I was doing work I found exciting, I had friends I thought liked me, cared about me. And then it all fell apart. I found myself in a police cell, my engagement off, Laura gone, being accused of attempted rape, and finding myself suddenly without any friends, not even you, Rae. No, I don't believe you have a clue how I feel.'

Rae looked uneasily at him. 'You'll get over this; work is what you need to help you forget. Maybe you should start work on the next set of illustrations sooner than we planned?'

'No,' Patrick said with force. 'I'm not working with you any more, Rae.'

'Don't be too hasty about this; you'll feel differently when you've had a few weeks to get over the shock.' Rae was still trying to tell him what he felt, what he thought.

He looked coolly at her. 'No, Rae. I have made up my mind.'

She went red then, angry and flustered. 'You can't break our contract, Patrick! The publishers wouldn't let you walk away. You have a legally binding contract for this series, remember!'

'If I had gone to prison for attempted rape, would you still have wanted me to illustrate your books?' he bit out. 'Would the publishers talk about legally binding contracts? Or would you all get the best possible lawyers to find a way of breaking our contract?'

Rae stared at him without answering. She didn't need to reply; they both knew what would have happened if he had been convicted.

'Goodbye, Rae.'

He turned and walked away, down the alleys and winding streets of Old Nice, towards the blinding blue of the Baie des Anges. He didn't know what he would do now. His future was utterly empty—without a job, without Laura, without any clear idea of what he wanted to do. All he knew was that he was angry; very angry. With Laura, with Rae, with fate, but most of all with that girl, Antonia Cabot.

He hoped he would never see her again, because if he did he wouldn't be responsible for his actions, and, just though he felt his rage to be, the girl had been through a terrible ordeal, too. Whatever her reasons for accusing him, whether it had been conscious resentment or unconscious hostility, she had suffered enough; he had to walk away and just shrug off his anger with her, which did not make it any easier to bear.

Bottled up and suppressed, his rage simmered inside him for the next two years, fed by his nightmares, by his new realisation of just how fragile was the identity, how easy to break.

He drew on the savings he had, studied art in Rome for a year, and then moved on to Florence to study there, living in the cheapest student accommodation, eating bread and cheese and fruit, drinking rough cheap wine, and earning some money at weekends by working in a bar at night, painting portraits of tourists in the streets by day.

One of his tutors got him a job each summer, during the vacations, in Venice, as a courier with an international holiday company, shepherding tourists around the city, helping them find postcards, and presents to take home, finding them when they got lost, and getting them where they had to be each day.

And then one day as summer ended, before art classes began again, he was on a *vaporetto* crossing the Grand Canal, from St Mark's square to the Accademia, where he meant to sit for an hour in front of the work of Giovanni Bellini, the artist he was concentrating on that week. He had his sketchpad under his arm, pencils, charcoal and crayons in his pockets; his mind was full of his favourite Bellini, the Virgin and child.

There was a little huddle of people on the *riva*, waiting for the *vaporetto* to arrive. Patrick idly glanced at them and then went rigid, staring.

Among them was Antonia Cabot.

There was no doubt about it, although she had changed. She didn't look so young any more; she didn't dazzle like a candle-flame. She was subdued, snuffed out, in a dark blue dress, cotton, a simple sleeveless tunic, and over that a short black cotton jacket.

Her pale gold hair had been cut very short, giving her the head of a boy; she had lost a lot of weight, was skinny, almost fleshless, and although this was a very hot summer she was pale, as if she rarely went out.

She was staring at the reflections on the water—the shimmering dancing images of churches, palaces, houses, rose-pink, aquamarine, cream.

As the *vaporetto* chugged slowly into place she stiffened, staring down at the reflection of it swimming towards her, the reflections of the faces of passengers. Of Patrick. Slowly, Antonia Cabot looked up, straight into Patrick's brooding eyes.

He grimly watched the last vestige of colour drain from her face, the stricken look come into it, the darkening of her sea-coloured eyes, the trembling of her generous mouth.

Then she turned and fled, away from the Accademia, up a side-street, her small black shadow running ahead of her on the painted walls.

Patrick had to wait until the *vaporetto* had docked and the barrier had been raised before he could jump ashore and set off after her.

# CHAPTER THREE

ANTONIA CABOT thought for a moment that she was seeing things. She stared down at the canal, watching his face quiver on the surface of the water.

It was the face she had seen so many times in nightmares, the face which had haunted her for the past two years. For a long time she had been afraid to go to sleep. She had sat up all night, heavy-eyed, white-faced, because she was afraid of meeting that face in her dreams.

Even now, although it happened less and less often, she still woke up shaking from one of those dreams every so often; and even when she was awake she wasn't safe; something would trigger a memory and she would catch herself thinking about him.

Frozen, she had stared at the reflection, expecting it to disappear any minute. But it hadn't. It had merely come closer, grown clearer.

Taking a deep breath, she had slowly looked up at last, and the hairs had risen on the back of her neck.

It wasn't her imagination. He was there, a few feet away, staring back.

She hadn't forgotten a detail of his face: the smooth brown hair, the threat of the brows over cold blue eyes, the strong nose, the mouth...

It was looking at that hard, angry mouth that ended her paralysis. She fled, bolted for home, like a hunted animal, getting curious looks from everyone she passed. It was rare to see anyone running in Venice. Tourists wandered along, staring; local people took their time too in that sultry summer heat. Antonia ran all out, hurled herself round the next corner, shot down an alley, through a shadowy court, across a bridge.

It was easy to lose yourself in Venice; there were so many ways to weave in and out between the blank-walled rear of buildings which faced the canals. It was a maze. Antonia already knew her way round it.

Instinctively as she ran she kept listening for the sound of following footsteps. Sound was magnified by high walls, by water; you could hear a whisper on a quiet day.

She heard the sound of running feet for the first couple of minutes, and then she shot across a bridge to the Rio San Vio, a wide pavement beside a canal, and doubled back again later, across another bridge, and emerged behind the Accademia.

By then, she was sure nobody was following her. She didn't slow down yet; she wanted to make quite sure she had lost him. Several streets away she halted at last, chest heaving, her body moist with perspiration, panting, in a small, empty square, listening, and heard nothing.

She had lost him. Walking unsteadily, she crossed the square, took a key from her pocket, unlocked a dark-varnished gate set in a high stone wall, and walked through into a shady green garden.

Nothing stirred there except a few birds, a whisper of leaves, a fountain splashing softly in the middle of the gravelled paths. She sat down on the stone wall around the fountain to get her breath back, and closed her eyes, shuddering.

He had changed; she couldn't quite pin down how, but he had looked very different. Yet she would have known him anywhere.

What was he doing in Venice?

She ran her trembling hands over her face, raked them through her short blonde hair. Was he just here for a day? A day tripper? Or was he staying here? What if she met him again?

Oh, God, she couldn't bear it if she did.

For two years she had been terrified of seeing him again, walking into him in a street somewhere, in a restaurant, an art gallery. The modern world was small; it was amazing how you did run into people you knew, in the strangest places. A friend of hers had been in the Hindu Kush when she ran into an ex-boyfriend, a thousand miles from where they had last met!

Antonia stared down into the water of the fountain; among the dark green leaves and huge white flowers of the water-lilies floating on the surface she saw his face again, and groaned, closing her eyes.

Desperately she dragged her sunglasses off, leaned down and put her face into the water, breaking up any reflections, cooling her overheated skin.

Dripping wet and refreshed, she sat up again, searching for a handkerchief in her jacket pocket, just as the gate creaked. Startled, she looked round, water clinging to her lashes, making a rainbow of light through which she saw him, standing in the open gateway.

Her heart plummeted, deeper than the ocean; she couldn't breathe, couldn't move.

She must have forgotten to lock the gate again in her relief at being safe home. She couldn't believe she had been so stupid!

White and terrified, she watched him, eyes stretched to their utmost, and couldn't even scream.

He came in. Shut the gate. Walked towards her, his black shadow thrown across the stone wall.

Shivering, in spite of the heat of the sun, she opened her mouth to scream, and he leapt across the space between them, his hand clamping down over her mouth to silence the cry before it came.

His blue eyes bored down into her. 'I'm not going to hurt you!' he grated, his teeth tight, and she didn't believe him. His face was taut with rage. 'Don't start screaming,' he bit out. 'I don't want to get arrested again because of you! Once was enough!'

Her enormous sea-blue eyes stared up at him, trying to read his intentions in his face, fear making her glossy black pupils dilate. He was standing in front of her, his thighs against her knees, his palm pressing down into her parted lips, his warm flesh touching the tip of her tongue. She tasted the salt on his skin and shuddered.

His mouth indented, he frowned. 'And stop looking at me like that! Do I really look like the type of guy who hurts women? I may have been as mad as hell with you two years ago, but I've had time to calm down. You're in no danger from me. Promise not to scream and I'll let go of you.' He paused. 'Nod your head if you promise.'

She couldn't swallow, was half suffocating; she nodded.

He released her and moved away a little, but was still too close; Antonia's heart was beating thickly in her throat.

Huskily she whispered, 'You must have been very angry, I know that, and I'm sorry I told the police it was you...'

His face tensed, his eyes glittering. 'So you did tell them it was me! You didn't just give them a description—you actually accused me!'

The harshness of his voice was more than she could take. She couldn't breathe; she was as cold as ice; the quiet garden began to dissolve in front of her terrified eyes.

She crumpled sideways a second later; Patrick only just caught her before she fell to the ground.

Her body sagged into his arms and he picked her up, thinking, She's as light as a child. Doesn't she eat at all? He carried her to an ornately wrought ironwork bench with wooden slats for a seat. Her blonde head lay against his arm, her short curls catching the light. He laid her down, went back to the fountain, damped his handkerchief in the water, then went back to her, knelt beside her, and gently stroked her temples with the cool, wet linen.

After a moment she shifted, frowning, her lids stirring, her lashes lifting, and looked up at him dazedly.

'You fainted,' he said.

She tried to sit up and he helped her, feeling her tense as he touched her.

'You don't have to be afraid of me,' he bit out. 'It wasn't me who attacked you, or aren't you still sure about that?'

A little dark red colour crept into her cheeks. 'I'm not afraid of you,' she denied, but it wasn't true. She was afraid, even though it had not been him who attacked her. She wasn't scared he would attack her; she was simply scared—of him, or of herself, perhaps? She didn't know.

She had been afraid for a long time now. It was a habit, hard to break. It had forced her life into a pattern she couldn't change.

'But you did think it was me,' he muttered in a curt voice. 'Why? In God's name what made you believe I'd do a thing like that?'

Stammering, she said, 'It was dark down on the beach, but his hair was the same colour as yours, and he had an English voice; and I'd just met you at the party, and I thought...' Her voice stopped dead; she took an audible breath.

'You thought?' he probed, frowning.

Their eyes met: hers wide, a darkened turquoise, the wet lashes curling back from them, his narrowed, hard, glittering blue.

She gave a faint wrenched sigh. 'When I spoke to you at the party you were so angry; you looked at me as if you hated me.'

He gave a rough sigh, rubbing a hand across the back of his neck as he felt the muscles in it tensing. 'Yes, I remember; I'm sorry, I was in a bad mood that night.'

'I know. My uncle saw what happened, and he came over and said I shouldn't take any notice because you were unhappy, your engagement had just been broken off. That's why...when I saw you walking down to the beach...why I followed you. I was worried about you. You looked so sad; I had some crazy idea I'd try to comfort you.' She stopped, a half-sob making her shake. 'And then...and that...that's why I thought it was you...who attacked me.'

'You put me through a couple of days of hell, do you know that?' Patrick suddenly said.

'I wasn't exactly having the time of my life myself!' Antonia threw back, a hectic flush in her cheeks.

Patrick reddened, too, his face tightening as if she had hit him. 'No, of course you weren't,' he muttered. 'I'm sorry; I don't know why I'm still so worked up about

it. I realise I should have forgotten about it by now, but
it hit me just at the wrong time. I was still reeling from
one shock when another one knocked me right off my
feet.' He angrily raked his hair back from his forehead.
'Look, it's very hot and I've walked a long way, following you; I need to sit down. Would you mind?' He
gestured to the seat beside her and Antonia hesitated,
biting her lip.

'There's nothing more to say, is there? I've told you
I'm sorry. I wasn't thinking straight when they inter-
viewed me; everything had got muddled up...' She broke
off, swallowing, her pale throat moving visibly. 'I know
it must have been painful for you, and I am sorry, believe me; what else can I say? It was two years ago. Can't
you just forget it?'

'Have you?' Patrick quietly asked, and her nervous
eyes fluttered a glance at his face, then away again. She
didn't answer; but she didn't have to.

Patrick sat down, turned sideways to half face her,
one arm going along the back of the seat, his long legs
stretched out. She was intensely conscious of him, which
appalled her. The strange, confusing similarity was still
there—the sound of his English voice, the gleam of his
hair, the way his body moved. She swung like a pen-
dulum all the time, between attraction and repulsion.

'Let's talk about something else,' he said in a casual
voice. 'What are you doing in Venice? Are you studying
here now?'

A fig tree grew close to the bench; Antonia kept her
eyes fixed on the tree's smooth grey patterned bark, the
shiny, deeply lobed green leaves; the sunlight pierced between them, made shifting patterns on the gravel underneath. Ever since she arrived at the house she had been
meaning to paint the tree, it was so beautiful. She

wouldn't paint it now; she wouldn't be able to bear to look at it; it would always remind her of these moments with Patrick.

'No,' she whispered. 'I went home as soon as the Italian police let me. I gave up my course in Florence, and went back to the States. I worked for my father, doing some research for a book he's been writing for years. He's an art historian, something of an authority on Jackson Pollock.' She gave Patrick a rapid glance. 'George Cabot? Have you heard of him?'

'George Cabot, yes, of course,' Patrick said, wondering if she was very proud of her father. The name did ring a bell, but he had never read any of the man's books; he wasn't into American modern art. He was too fixated on the Italian Renaissance; it left no room for other art. 'Are both your parents still alive?'

'Yes,' Antonia said. She had seen more of her father during those months when she worked for him than she had ever seen before, but she hadn't got to know him any better. An almost silent man, George Cabot lived and breathed his work and had never had much time or attention to spare for his wife or daughter. He was too remote; obsessed with his own interior life, he tried to be kind, tried to be understanding, but he kept forgetting her and drifting off, back into his preferred world.

Her mother, Annette Cabot, was just as busy, just as remote, in another way. All she cared about was her social life. She worked for local charities, sat on committees, and lunched and dined with important and influential people.

Antonia's parents were alive, but separated from her by a barrier almost as strong as death: indifference.

Patrick, watching her pale face, wondered what she was thinking about to give that sadness to her eyes. The way they had met, the trauma, for both of them, which had marked that meeting, had forged a strange, subterranean link between them. He had thought about her all the time over the past two years; he was intensely curious about her, even more so now that he had seen her again. She was so fragile, with her light, fluttering hair and her sad eyes. He kept wanting to touch her; but that would be madness. This was not a girl you could risk touching, not any more. He sensed that the merest touch of a hand would make her terrified. She was like a wild bird in a cage, ready to dash itself to death against the bars if a hand reached out to it.

Carefully, keeping his voice casual, he asked, 'Who do you take after—your father or your mother?'

'Neither,' Antonia said, but it wasn't quite true. She was a mixture of them both. She inherited her colouring from her mother. Annette Cabot was a beautiful woman, blonde and classically elegant, blue-eyed, a little icy. Antonia inherited her artistic talent from her father, and her shyness.

She had been sent away to school at an early age, had spent her vacations in summer school or been sent on skiing holidays in winter, and then, when she was eighteen, had been sent to Italy to study art.

All Antonia's friends had said she was lucky—Italy alone, with every chance of having fun! Wow, they had said, her parents were great, letting her go so far away. But they hadn't understood. She had been far away all her life.

Her parents were never unkind; they were charming to her, generous, took care that she had what she wanted, but Antonia had known in her heart of hearts that they did not love her.

She was an interruption to their otherwise important lives, and although, for a short while after she came home from Italy two years ago, they had tried hard to bridge the gap between her and them, appalled and overwhelmed by what had happened to her, by then it had been too late. Antonia had not wanted them.

She had retreated into silence herself; small and pale and needing only to avoid being noticed, she had put up a barrier nobody could cross, and slowly her parents had given up, drifted back to their own lives, their own obsessions.

Antonia had been left alone with her claustrophobic dreams, her haunted days and nights. She had stopped eating; she was shrinking, slowly turned into a ghost of herself.

Then her mother's brother, Uncle Alex, had come to visit, had taken one look at her and been horrified. 'You can't go on like this!' he had said. 'You've lost so much weight you look like a child of twelve! And that's how you're dressing, too. My God, can't you see what you're doing to yourself? You're trying to pretend it never happened; you've gone back into childhood to escape it. You've got arms and legs like little sticks; you're anorexic. Now don't lie about it! I've got eyes in my head; I can see it. If your parents weren't so obsessed with themselves, they would see it, too. We're going to have to do something about it. You must confront it, go back to Italy, face up to what happened.'

'No, I can't!' she had said, white-faced, and gone on saying it for weeks, but Uncle Alex was dogged. He wouldn't take no for an answer, and eventually he had talked her on to the plane, back to Florence, to pick up her studies again.

Her parents had approved, relieved to see her go. With her out of sight and far away they needn't feel they should be worrying about her, doing something about her. They needn't feel guilty any more.

That was one reason why she had come back to Italy, in fact—so that her parents need not look so uneasy when they saw her, so that they need not feel guilty. Her other reason was Uncle Alex's distress at the sight of her. He made her feel he cared.

'What are you thinking about to make you look like that?' Patrick asked, and she started.

'Nothing.'

He knew she lied, and watched her, his blue eyes narrowed. He wished he could see inside her head, but maybe he would hate what he saw. Something terrible must have happened to this girl to make her look the way she did.

'So when did you come back to Italy?' he asked, and she sighed.

'Uncle Alex and Susan-Jane rented a flat in Florence for six months, and I shared it with them, and finished my art course. Then when their lease ran out they left and I stayed on, in a smaller flat somewhere else.'

They had made her go to classes, filled the flat with people, got her eating again—lots of pasta with cream and eggs—had stayed until they were certain that Antonia was going to be able to manage on her own. Nobody in Florence had known about what had happened to her; that had made it easier, and being away from her parents had helped too. Uncle Alex and Susan-Jane cared about her, and that had worked a sort of magic.

'They're great,' she said. 'I love Uncle Alex, and Susan-Jane is great fun, not like an aunt, more like a sister.'

Patrick remembered the cartoonist's face in the villa that night as the police were hustling him past the open door into the huge lounge. If Alex Holtner could have got his hands on him at that moment he would have killed him, he thought. Yes, Alex Holtner loved his niece, no doubt about that.

'Do they still live in Bordighera?'

'No, they sold that villa; they bought a big three-bedroomed flat in Monte Carlo—that's their home base now—but they're born wanderers; they travel all the time, right around the world, because, of course, Uncle Alex can work anywhere. He's been working here—he rented this house for the summer.'

Patrick gazed at the little strawberry-pink-painted house with its white ironwork balcony over which a white awning stretched, shading the windows on the upper floor of the house, and coveted it. He was living in a tiny flat high up in a shabby old house, in a back street of Cannaregio, a district where once the canal had wound between tall green bamboo canes, long since vanished.

His room was filled with a smell of cooking from the flats below, overrun with bugs of one kind or another, swelteringly hot during the day and stuffy at night.

'Lucky Uncle Alex, nice to be a rich cartoonist,' he drily said. 'It's beautiful. Are they here now?'

She hesitated, her lashes drooping over her eyes, half tempted to lie, then shook her head, but didn't tell him that Alex and Susan-Jane were not even in Venice, that they had flown to London to have a business meeting with Alex's agent, who was visiting England. They had invited Antonia to go, too, but she had decided to stay and have a few quiet days alone.

'Probably just as well,' Patrick grimaced. 'The last time I saw him he looked as if he would like to kill me.'

She bit her lip. 'I'm sorry, I'm afraid he was very angry, and he's always wished he had had a chance to say sorry to you, but you left without going back to the villa.'

'Yes, I felt it would be wiser—I was pretty sore about the whole episode at the time. I might have turned nasty if I had run into your uncle; I was in no mood to accept apologies.'

Antonia gave him a searching sideways look. 'Why did you break your contract with Rae Dunhill? I felt awful about that—it wasn't her fault!'

He groaned. 'I must admit, I regretted that afterwards. I had always liked Rae, and I enjoyed working with her—but she had believed I was guilty, and I found that hard to forgive; I felt I never wanted to see her again. It takes a long time to get over these things.'

'Yes,' she said, and they both stared at each other in silence, around them the tranquillity of the garden, of the streets surrounding it.

This district of Venice was called the Dorsoduro, which meant 'hard-back'; built on a hard clay base, it was a labyrinth of winding little streets, full of small private houses, built for workers long ago, later inhabited by the English during the period when there was a large English colony in Venice. The area stretched between the Accademia and the church of Santa Maria della Salute, which was the first glimpse of Venice to greet returning ships.

Patrick dragged his gaze away from Antonia and looked around the garden. 'It's so quiet here; you would think this was a country area, instead of being the middle of Venice! How much longer will you all be staying here?'

'A few more weeks, that's all. I shall be sorry to leave.' She had the strangest sensation; she couldn't believe she

was really here, in this tranquil little paradise, with the
man who had haunted her for two years. She had been
so terrified of seeing him again. Yet here they were sitting
under the fig tree with the gentle, musical splash of the
fountain to keep them company, talking quietly, and she
didn't feel afraid any more.

Except . . . except that every moment or so she would
look at him and feel herself shrink, as if from the touch
of fire. It hadn't been this man who had attacked her,
yet she found it hard not to keep confusing the two of
them. Their faces shifted, changed places all the time in
her mind, as the leaves on the fig tree moved, flickering
dark flames of shadow which were never still, could not
be counted.

'And then you go back to Florence?' he asked.

She shook her head. 'No, I've finished my course
there. I've got a job.' She stopped, said wryly, 'Well,
Uncle Alex got me a job. Cataloguing a private collection—have you heard of Patsy Devvon? She's the
widow of Gus Devvon; his family made early radios, but
he sold out of the company and invested his money in
computers, I gather.' She could talk to him freely about
the Devvons; the subject was impersonal; it unlocked
her tongue; she talked fast, lightly. 'When he retired he
came over to Europe, settled here in Venice, and spent
years buying things—paintings, sculpture, books, even
early radios and gramophones and recordings. It's all in
a hideous muddle; things got piled into rooms on the
upper floor of this *palazzo* where they lived. The floor
was never used and is very damp, the plaster is cracked
and crumbling on the ceilings and the paintwork is blis-
tering, there's mould and fungus growing on things . . .
It's such a mess.'

Patrick watched her with very clear, thoughtful blue eyes. She had looked so different, talking like that, her face mobile, changing, full of life.

'So you'll stay on in Venice after the lease of this house runs out? Alone?'

She flushed slightly, looking down, and nodded.

His eyes narrowed. What did that look mean? He was beginning to recognise her expressions; the fragile mobility of her face was self-betraying. She was hiding something, or not telling him something. But what?

'Will you try and find another flat, or stay on in a pension?' he asked.

Another of those tell-tale hesitations. She was reluctant to tell him anything about herself, but his level stare somehow forced her to answer in the end.

'I've been invited to move into the *palazzo* until I've finished my work.' Then, quickly, she added, 'I'll be sorry to leave this house. I've loved living here. The house is small, but cosy, and gardens are so rare in Venice; this one is like a dream.'

He let his gaze wander around from the pink house to the fig tree, an olive tree growing nearer the house, roses climbing on the walls, orange trees, swaddled like babies, in straw matting, standing in huge terracotta pots along the wall of the house.

'Beautiful,' he agreed. 'That fig is covered with fruit; I've always wanted to have my own fig tree and be able to pick them when I wanted them.'

'Have one,' she offered, smiling. 'There are so many; we'll only eat a few.'

'May I really?' He smiled, stood up, and broke off one of the plump, pear-shaped, ridged fruit which took two years to ripen from green to that rich, luscious purplish black.

Sitting down again, Patrick used his thumbnail to break open the fig, and they both stared at the glistening greeny pink seeds inside.

Patrick broke off one half, offered it to her. Antonia lifted it to her mouth, her white teeth visible as she ate some of the sweet interior, and Patrick did the same, then stiffened, his eyes fixed on her left hand.

'Is that an engagement ring?'

Antonia pulled her hand down to her side, as if to hide it. The fig fell out of her fingers and rolled under the bench.

Patrick leaned over and seized her hand, lifted it to stare at the enormous diamond surrounded by a circle of smaller ones in an elaborate platinum setting.

'When did this happen?'

'I got engaged last month.' Her voice was a mere thread of sound, with a faint tremor in it.

He was frightening her again. That look was back in his face—a harshness that disturbed her. Why was he looking at her like that? As if she had done something wrong? Then she thought, And why do I feel so guilty? Why didn't I want him to know?

'Who is he?' Patrick's voice was curt. Seeing the ring on her finger had knocked him off balance. That was the last thing he would ever have expected, that Antonia Cabot might be planning to get married.

He was angry, too, although he didn't know why he was. Maybe because this had upset all his beliefs about her? He was puzzled. Antonia did not look like a girl who was blissfully in love and couldn't wait to get married. In fact Antonia Cabot looked like a wraith, afraid of everything, but especially of men.

'His name is Cy,' she whispered.

'Is what?'

'Cy—short for Cyrus,' she said. 'Cyrus Devvon. Mrs Devvon's nephew, or, rather, her late husband's nephew.'

Patrick's brows met. 'That's the owner of the *palazzo*?'

'Yes.'

'Is that where you met him?'

'Yes.' Her sea-blue eyes were lowered, her darkened lashes shifting and flickering nervously.

'He lives there too?'

'He's in the States at the moment, but he'll be back next month, for a few weeks.'

'What does he do for a living, or is he too rich to work?' Patrick's mouth twisted in cynicism, and she resented that look.

'He's an accountant; he has a practice in Boston. He looks after the family money—Mrs Devvon lives on the interest from all her late husband's shares. The capital is tied up in a trust fund, and will all pass to Cy when his aunt dies. His firm administers the estate.'

'A very wealthy accountant, then,' Patrick said, smiling at her sardonically. 'Well, congratulations. What's he like? Is he good-looking as well as rich? A real Prince Charming, I hope?'

The sarcasm made her cross. There was a fine gold chain around her throat, disappearing into the neckline of her dark blue dress. Looking down, she pulled the chain upwards, but it had caught on something on the inside of her dress. Flushed, she tugged unavailingly.

'Here, let me do it,' Patrick said impatiently, pushing her hand aside, and then, before she could stop him, had hooked one long finger down inside her dress.

Hot colour flowed up her face; she began breathing raggedly, and tried to push his hand away, but Patrick had already freed the small object on the end of the chain which had lodged itself inside her bra. He deftly fished it out and pulled it into view.

'Is that what you were looking for?'

Her hand shook as she took it from him, not looking at him.

Patrick watched her, narrow-eyed. It had been a calculated risk to steal that small intimacy. He had wondered how she would react; it had been a litmus test and he was sure now that he was right. He had felt the panic rising in her; under his searching finger he had felt her heart fluttering like a trapped bird. His first impression of her had been all too accurate. What had happened to her in Bordighera had scared her into withdrawal from life, and especially from any contact with men. Which made him all the more puzzled to be told she was planning to get married.

She opened the gold locket with shaky difficulty; not looking at him, she held it out.

'That's Cy.'

Patrick looked at the small photograph intently. It was a picture of Antonia with a man in a lightweight white suit and an open-necked shirt. He was tall and thin, with a narrow face, dark eyes and pale hair.

'He's old enough to be your father!' Patrick said.

Flushed, she snapped, 'He's only in his thirties!'

'Late thirties, then, very late,' Patrick said drily. 'Why are you marrying him?'

Antonia stared at him in bewilderment.

'W...why? Well, obviously——'

'Nothing obvious about it,' Patrick coolly told her. 'And don't tell me you're in love—I don't believe it. For one thing, he's much too old for you, and, for another, your reaction just now when I helped you fish this locket out of your dress told me that you still go into panic every time a man comes near you.'

Resentment in her voice, she snapped, 'You know nothing about me! You have a nerve, talking to me like that! And you had a nerve putting your hand inside my dress—if you ever do that again I'll hit you with something hard!'

He gave her a wry smile. 'You're just trying to shout me down, don't think I don't know that. You don't want me telling you the truth, but I'm going to, anyway. You aren't in love—with this guy or anybody else.'

'Of course you know me so well that you can tell at sight, without ever having even met Cy!'

The heavy sarcasm simply made him laugh. 'I've seen what he looks like, and I can guess why you've got engaged. I can read you like a book. He's your security blanket, isn't he? You aren't in love with him; you've picked him because you hope he'll take care of you without making too many personal demands on you. He doesn't look as if he has much of a sex drive——'

'Oh...shut up...' she furiously said, her colour coming and going, first scarlet then white.

Patrick merely went on calmly, 'I don't suppose he has ever tried to get you into bed.'

She leapt up and made for the house, running; but Patrick caught her by the fountain and held her by the waist, pushing her backwards up against the stone basin, holding her there, standing in front of her, his body not quite touching hers.

Her agitated eyes flickered up to his face and away. 'Don't...' she whispered, her voice shaking. 'Please don't...'

He stopped smiling and looked at her impatiently. 'How many times do I have to tell you? I won't hurt you!'

'Then let go of me!'

Calmly and coaxingly, Patrick said, 'Come on, do you really think I might attack you? Do I look the type?'

She broke out in a wail, like a scared child. 'No, I know, but... oh, I don't know how to explain... I... I get... I get the two of you mixed up, in my head...'

He froze, staring down at her, face rigid. 'You still confuse me with that bastard? Thanks.'

'I'm sorry,' she said wearily.

He went on staring, his brows together, then suddenly broke out roughly, 'Have you any idea what you look like? I remember you that night, at the party, when you were dancing... You were lit up like a Christmas tree; you sparkled and glittered. Look at you now; you're like a ghost! What are you trying to do to yourself?'

She was leaning backwards, to get as far away from him as possible, deeply aware of his lean, supple body, the tanned skin of face and throat, the hard male mouth talking to her with such incisive scorn.

'I'm trying to get my life together again!' she threw back at him, and his blue eyes flashed.

'Is that why you're wearing that boring dress, that shapeless jacket? And the body under them could be a boy's; you don't even look like a woman any more! Your lovely hair has all been cut off; you aren't wearing make-up. You look terrible!'

'Leave me alone!' she broke out, resenting that description of herself. 'It's my life, not yours. You don't have to live inside my head, so stay out of it. Please just go away and don't come back!'

Her voice rose fiercely on the final words, and all the birds in the garden took fright at the sound, and clattered up into the burning blue sky, their wings sunlit.

At the same instant, she gave him a shove and he stumbled and fell across the edge of the fountain into the water.

He pulled himself upwards again, dripping wet; but she had gone; he saw her running between green leaves and white roses, then she was at the house and vanished into it with a slam of a door.

Patrick pushed his wet hair back from his face, dried himself as much as possible with his damp handkerchief, and a moment later left by the gate in the garden wall. He was going, but he would be back.

# CHAPTER FOUR

ANTONIA watched Patrick leave, from an upstairs window in the house. She was still trembling, but as soon as he had gone she ran back downstairs, out into the garden, and made sure this time that the gate was locked. Patrick Ogilvie wasn't getting in again.

She went back into the house and rang the *palazzo*. Mrs Devvon's maid, Lucia, answered.

'You are late. What has happened? She thinks you had an accident. You know what she's like; she is getting upset.'

'Tell her I'm very sorry, but I can't come today; I'm sick,' Antonia said huskily. It wasn't entirely a lie; she felt as if she might throw up at any minute. She was feverish, shaky, cold sweat dewing her forehead.

'Why didn't you phone earlier?' Lucia was a small, dark woman in her fifties with sharp black eyes, weathered olive skin, and black hair slowly turning grey, who had worked for Mrs Devvon for nearly twenty years.

'I set out, then felt so sick, I had to go back,' Antonia said uneasily. She found it hard to lie. 'Tell Mrs Devvon that I'm sure I'll be better tomorrow.'

Lucia grunted. 'Huh.'

Antonia flushed guiltily, knowing Lucia guessed she wasn't telling the truth. But she couldn't have gone to the *palazzo* today, pretended to be normal, talked to Mrs Devvon as if nothing had happened. She knew the turmoil inside her would have shown in her face.

She rang off and lay down on her bed, aware of the house empty and silent around her, and beyond that the dusty little square, the quiet streets. It was like being on a desert island.

A local woman came in three times a week to clean, but she wouldn't be coming today. Antonia wouldn't have to pretend everything was just wonderful, when, in fact, the sky had just fallen in on her.

She had hoped she would never see him again. She was still dazed with the shock of recognising his face on the waters of the Grand Canal. It had been a surreal moment—incredible, terrifying.

She curled up into a foetal position, her arms clasped round her knees, shivering. He might have gone now, but he would come back. She knew it. She had thought she was getting over it, that it had faded like a bruise, all but disappeared. Seeing him today had brought it all back, though. The nightmare pressed at the borders of her mind, and she was afraid of falling asleep again.

Just now, for instance, when he'd touched her, pushed his finger down inside her dress, she had felt dizzy; she felt her heart pick up speed now at the very memory.

Her skin burned; she shut her eyes. No! She mustn't think about that.

But she couldn't shut it out of her head. It kept returning—the intense sensation when his finger slid down the cleft between her breasts, his skin cool, yet leaving such heat everywhere it touched.

It had all happened in a second. He had been quick to disengage the locket, yet to her it had seemed an endless time; it had seemed to happen in slow motion. The tiny golden hairs on her skin had been drawn upwards to his flesh, as if he magnetised them. Her nerve-endings had gone on vibrating after his finger moved away. She had felt every sensation with such incredible intensity.

Even remembering it was unbearable.

She put her hands over her face, groaning. Ever since that night on the beach she had been terrified of any sort of intimacy, mental or physical. She preferred to keep people at a distance, shut them out, hide from them. In the garden just now, though, Patrick Ogilvie had invaded her head, as well as her body space; he had touched her, in some way or another, over and over again, probing her mind, asking her questions she did not want to answer, picking up every instinct of her senses.

She didn't know which was worse—the mental or the physical invasions. They had only been together in the garden for such a short time, yet she couldn't count the number of ways he had come too close. He had carried her in his arms when she fainted. She had woken up to find him holding her, his body touching hers, his face bending over her. Later he had slid that cool finger down inside her dress and she had felt him watching her while he did that, assessing her reactions.

His blue eyes were so quick and shrewd; at times she had felt as if they could see right through her, read her thoughts—and she hadn't only imagined it, because later he had actually said so, said he could tell what she was feeling, guess what she was thinking.

He had made her angry, frightened her, worried her— in half an hour he had come closer to her in every possible way than anyone else had ever done over the past two years, and Antonia found that deeply disturbing.

She left for the *palazzo* earlier than usual next day and was out until late in the afternoon. If Patrick Ogilvie

had been to the house in the interim she saw no sign of
it. He would have found nobody in if he had come, and
the house would have been well locked up.

She had been very busy all day, sorting through a large
trunk containing the usual muddle of objects—some very
valuable books had been pushed in with a set of eight-
eenth-century Chinese plates, several early wax cylinder
recordings, a portfolio of Victorian anatomical drawings
of horses, dogs and other animals, thought to be by
Munnings, business papers and letters.

Patsy Devvon came down to look at them, drifting
into the room in a blue silk harem suit, a flowing jacket
over trousers that ballooned at the thigh then came in
and were tied at the ankle. It suited her; she had an un-
erring sense of what did suit her. In her forties, very
slim, relentlessly dieting all the time, with pale blue eyes
and hair she now had to dye to keep it blonde, she looked
far younger than her age, and dressed to maintain the
illusion.

'I've no idea where all that came from,' she said,
peering at the piles of objects Antonia had laid out on
a table. 'Where's the trunk they were in?' She inspected
that, saw a torn label on one side. 'I think we bought
that at an auction in Paris,' she said. 'Yes, that address
is a French one, that's the auctioneer's address. Gus was
always buying stuff when we were away, and having it
freighted here. He loved the flea market in Paris, could
never resist browsing around the stalls and buying lots
of that old junk. Is any of this valuable?'

'I think the wax cylinders are probably the most
valuable; they're very rare, and I can't play them to find
out who is on them, because we would need the right
machine for that, but if they are recordings of someone
famous they could be worth more than any of these other

things. We'll have to have them assessed by an expert, which I'm not.'

'But you're so clever even knowing what they are,' Patsy said, picking up one of the cylinders and turning it around, staring at it curiously. 'I wouldn't have had a clue, honey. Funny-looking things, aren't they?'

She had been Gus Devvon's fourth wife, and years younger than her husband, who had been sixty when he married Patsy. Gus had collected women, as he collected *objets d'art*; none of his previous wives had lasted very long—he had lost interest in them quite fast—but his marriage to Patsy had lasted nearly twenty years, until his death, and although Antonia hadn't known Mr Devvon she could understand how Patsy had held him longer than any of his previous wives. She was a lively, warm-hearted, friendly woman and Antonia was very fond of her. So was Cy. Patsy was as close as a sister to him, and she had welcomed Antonia into their family.

'Well, you deal with it, honey,' she told Antonia, smiling vaguely as she drifted away again. 'I'm off to lunch with Amy Patterson; see you later.'

Antonia had her lunch on a tray in the dusty, echoing cavern of a room she was working in on the top floor of the old building. It was a simple meal: melon, followed by pasta with a bacon and mushroom sauce. Lucia came to get the tray later and lingered to inspect what Antonia had been doing so far.

'What rubbish that man bought! I would just throw it out if I had my way!'

'Then you'd be throwing away large sums of money,' Antonia told her, and was amused by the quick, sharp look she got.

'It's really valuable? All that dusty old stuff?'

'What you see on the table is worth thousands, at least,' Antonia assured her, and Lucia pulled a face.

'Crazy.' She picked up the tray, stared at the half-eaten pasta. 'You didn't even touch any of this!'

'I did; it was lovely,' Antonia hurriedly said. 'But there was far too much for me.'

'You don't eat enough to keep a mouse alive! No wonder you're so pale and skinny. I can't think what Mr Cy sees in you. What he needs is a woman with red blood in her veins, not a pallid little thing like you.'

Lucia was not only Mrs Devvon's maid; she ran the house with a rod of iron. There were several other servants who cleaned and cooked; Lucia gave them their orders and kept a beady eye on them, as she did on Antonia, and she believed she had the right to comment on anything that concerned the Devvon family.

Antonia bit her lip and didn't retort. Lucia gave her a grim little smile of satisfaction, and shuffled away again. Antonia got on with her work, feeling oddly uneasy all the time, wishing Cy would ring. He made her feel so safe.

Safe. Her smile vanished; her face stiffened and paled. Patrick Ogilvie had tarnished the word 'safe' now; she would be afraid to use it because he had given it a new implication, insinuated that the warm feeling of being secure and cherished she had when Cy was with her was somehow false, unreal.

Why should it be wrong to want to feel safe? She had never felt that way before with anyone. Her parents had always excluded her from their lives; from childhood she had felt like an outsider, her nose pressed against the window of life, watching enviously as other people enjoyed happiness and security. Hers had been such a strange childhood. She had only been happy when Uncle

Alex and Susan-Jane were around; they gave her the illusion of happy family life.

She had been very happy on the night of that barbecue party at the villa in Bordighera. Everyone was so friendly, and there were plenty of people of her own age. She had been having a great time, dancing, talking, listening to the music, and then she had seen Patrick Ogilvie standing not far away, watching her intently.

Her heart had missed a beat. She had been deaf, dumb, blind to everything else around her for a moment, staring back.

He was the most exciting man she had ever seen—tall, with a lean, supple body and golden tanned skin, those startling blue eyes, and sun-bleached brown hair which tumbled down over his temples. She couldn't stop staring at him, breathless at his looks, full of curiosity about him.

Was he an actor? With looks like that he could be. A pity he was so much older. He must be thirty or so, she decided, way out of her league, especially with that faintly grim look about him. But she rather liked the grimness; it gave him a dangerous air. He wouldn't be as easy to get on with as any of the boys she had been dancing with. She had the distinct impression he was angry about something; there was a darkness deep in those blue eyes.

She waited for him to turn away, look at other girls, but he hadn't. He had gone on staring at her, so fixedly that she had felt excitement running through her like fire through her veins.

He couldn't really be interested in her, could he? she had thought incredulously. Could he?

She had begun to smile shyly, and then his face had changed. His mouth had twisted impatiently; he had frowned, turned away, drained the glass of red wine he was holding and put the glass down on the nearest table, his whole body tense and restless.

Antonia remembered now how her heart had sunk. He was turning away. He was going to walk off and ask somebody else to dance. But why had he stared at her with such attention, then lost interest? Maybe he had decided she was too young? There was a big gap in their ages, after all. Maybe he was shy, reluctant to ask her to dance in case she rejected him as too old?

She couldn't just let him go like that. Urgency had given her an unusual courage; she had gone over to him, nerving herself to make the first approach.

Very unsure of herself and yet very excited, her heart beating thickly in her throat, she had asked him to dance.

He had turned, his face blank, stared down at her without answering, as if he had never seen her before.

At close hand he was even better looking than she had thought at first. Antonia had moved closer, wondering if he didn't understand English, had put a hand on his sleeve, given him a shy smile, not quite able to meet his eyes, hoping he could not see the tell-tale pulses she felt beating in her throat. Just touching his arm had sent her temperature way up.

And then he had rejected her, his voice a slap in the face. 'I don't dance,' he had said, eyes dismissive, and walked away.

She had gone scarlet, then white, wanting to cry but unable to in front of all those people. She had blundered away, like a moth flapping into a window, blinded by a flame which had singed its wings.

She remembered people moving apart as she almost cannoned into them, was horrified to realise that the little incident had been noticed, that her humiliation had had an audience.

Uncle Alex caught up with her, put an arm round her, and steered her into a shady corner where they wouldn't be overheard.

'Are you OK, honey? What did Patrick say to make you look like that?'

She had been too close to tears to answer and he had sighed, watching her face.

'You mustn't take it too seriously, whatever it was—he's feeling very low tonight; his engagement has just been broken off.' He had given her a glass of wine, told her all about Patrick Ogilvie and his fiancée, Laura, who had left him for another man, and Antonia had listened intently, understanding then why Patrick had behaved that way with her.

He had been hurt, he was angry, in no mood to get involved with another woman, and who could blame him? Her heart had filled with sympathy and pity; she had ached to do something for him, make him smile again, if only for a moment.

She had looked around to find him and seen him leaving the party, wandering off through the garden in the direction of the beach, his face moody, body wearily graceful under his elegant casual clothes.

'Come and dance with me,' Uncle Alex had invited her, but she had refused, saying she would rather just wander round and talk to people.

In fact, she had already made up her mind to follow Patrick. Maybe if he talked about his feelings it might help? she had thought hopefully. Perhaps he'd be glad of a sympathetic ear? Oh, she had found it easy to think of reasons for going after him; you could always find excuses for doing what you badly want to do.

She had slipped away down to the beach, and seen the track of his footsteps in the sand. Childishly, she had walked in his footprints, which were so much larger than her own, placing her feet carefully where his had trod, looking along the darkened beach, listening to the sound the waves made grating on pebbles, the slow whisper of the tide withdrawing again.

She had been so engrossed with thinking of Patrick that she hadn't heard a sound before someone leapt out at her, from behind a beached boat. She had had just that one brief glimpse, seen tanned skin, moonlight on light brown hair. She had tried to cry out, been silenced, heard an English voice angrily threaten her, and been sure it was him.

As he forced her down on to the sand she had fought desperately, shocked and terrified, while in her head she had thought, Does he think that this is why I followed him? Does he think I want this?

Even more disturbing was the fact that she couldn't stop herself thinking, too, Did I want him to make love to me? Was that why I followed him down here? Have I asked for this? Invited it? Is it my fault this is happening to me?

When the sound of voices had made him stop and she was left alone, weeping, in pain and misery, she had crawled into the clean salt sea and been half tempted to let herself be washed away on the outgoing tide. But something stronger than she knew, deep inside her, an anger against the man who had done this to her, a life force which would not give in, had dragged her up out of the sea, just as Uncle Alex had come looking for her.

Susan-Jane had noticed her long absence from the party, had been concerned enough to ask if Alex knew where she was, and people had started looking for her, calling her name in the garden, along the beach. The sound of their voices had frightened her attacker away, she realised later.

Uncle Alex had found her staggering up towards the villa, bleeding and weeping. She remembered his stunned white face, his anger, as he'd got out of her what had happened, wrapped her in a towel, and taken her into the villa, where the police and doctor were called.

'Who did this to you?' Uncle Alex had asked.

'The Englishman...' she had wept, not even remembering his name in her confused condition. 'It was him...the Englishman...'

'Englishman?' Uncle Alex had asked. 'Do you mean Ogilvie?'

'Yes,' she had said, and again, when the police asked, 'Do you mean Mr Patrick Ogilvie?' she had repeated it.

'Yes, it was him.'

She had been so sure.

Afterwards, when they had told her it had been someone else, it had not been Patrick Ogilvie, she had felt a bewildering mix of reaction—relief, that he hadn't hurt her like that, after all; shock, because it had been some total stranger and her view of what had happened had changed again; and eventually distress because of what she began to realise she had put Patrick through.

'He must hate me,' she had said to Uncle Alex.

'It was an honest mistake; you can't be blamed,' her uncle had soothed, but she had not been comforted.

She knew Patrick must hate her, especially when she heard that he had left Bordighera without even going back to the villa to collect his things, and, later, that he had walked out of his contract to illustrate Rae Dunhill's books because he was so angry with Rae for having been ready to believe he had attacked Antonia.

She had seen Rae briefly before she, too, left Bordighera. 'I feel very badly about having accused your friend,' Antonia had whispered, and Rae had given an impatient little shrug.

'Oh, nobody blames you,' she had said flatly. 'Don't worry about it. From what the police have said, it sounds as if the real guy did look vaguely like Patrick.'

Antonia had suppressed an instinctive shudder of re-action at that, hating the thought; but Rae Dunhill hadn't seemed to notice the change in her expression.

She had been too busy talking. 'It's just a pity it happened now, at this particular moment in his life. Patrick was already off balance after his engagement was suddenly broken off. That hit him hard; I'm afraid this has been the last straw. I went over to see him the other day, and hardly recognised him. He was always such an easy-going, reasonable guy. You could always talk to Patrick—he was never difficult; I could always get him to do what I wanted—but out of the blue he told me he wouldn't work with me again, he was backing out of his contract. At first I didn't believe he meant it, but suddenly he's like granite. I actually felt quite nervous of him, he's so different.'

Antonia had winced, filled with guilt, knowing that all this was her fault. 'What is he going to do instead, then?' she had asked miserably. 'How will he earn a living?'

'Oh, I gather he has quite a bit in the bank—he had been saving for a long time, to buy a house after he and Laura were married. He can live on that for some time, and I'm sure he'll get lots of work elsewhere. He's always been very successful. That's what's so maddening. I don't want to lose him; he's the best illustrator I've ever worked with.' Rae had sighed heavily, impatiently. 'But I got nowhere when I tried to talk him round, he was adamant, and—do you know?—I was actually afraid to go on arguing with him. I got the feeling I would be sorry if I did.' Rae had made a wry face at her. 'And I'm not normally the nervous type with men. I wouldn't have believed Patrick could change that way.'

Antonia had been wondering if she should write to him to tell him she was sorry, or maybe even try to see him, but after listening to Rae she had been scared of facing him again, and during the last two years she had always felt a leap of alarm and agitation whenever she thought of him.

Now she had met him, talked to him, and at one and the same time it had been both worse, and easier, than she had anticipated. He had been very angry at first; there had been explosive rage in his face, in the way he moved. After she had fainted, though, he seemed to have calmed down. He talked quietly, conversationally, as if they were mere acquaintances—until he saw her engagement ring, and then he changed again. Why had he been so angry when he'd found out she was engaged?

She had thought herself round in a circle, was back where she had started, facing the fact that Patrick Ogilvie still haunted her and she still didn't understand him.

She warily approached the house on the Dorsoduro that evening, making sure Patrick wasn't around before she unlocked the gate in the wall and walked through the garden to the back of the house.

She ate some salad for her evening meal, with freshly bought Italian bread, followed by a peach which she peeled and ate listening to local radio, the current top twenty hits, humming along with those she knew quite well.

She opened a can of cat food after that and went out to call the half-wild cats which lived in the garden shed, but were not allowed indoors. They warily approached, tails up, hissed at each other as they began to wolf down their food.

While she was watching them, she heard a thud in the garden, then a rustling, followed by another, unmistakable sound.

Footsteps grating on the gravel.

The hair rose on the back of Antonia's neck. She turned hurriedly, her heart racing so fast that she felt sick.

She knew before she saw him that it was Patrick. He loped towards her, a darker shadow in the gathering dusk, like a wolf coming down on the fold, a tall man wearing black jeans and a thin black summer shirt, open at the throat.

She was so taken by surprise that she didn't even think of running back indoors before he reached her.

'How did you get in?' she attacked as he confronted her.

'Climbed over the wall,' he coolly admitted, staring down at her, his blue eyes wandering over the lilac cotton tunic dress she wore.

'That's burglary!' she accused, wishing he would not look at her that way. His blue eyes dismissed her dress as dull, which it was; but she didn't want men staring. She wanted to walk the streets of Venice without being noticed, and in this very simple dress she did.

'You can't burgle someone's garden!' he drawled.

'Illegal entry, then,' she furiously said and, as he opened his mouth as if to argue, raised her voice and shouted him down. 'Well, whatever you call it, I'm going to ring the police if you don't leave at once. I don't want you on my property!'

'This isn't your property, though, is it? Your uncle has a short-term lease, that's all.'

'Why don't you go away and leave me alone?' raged Antonia, wishing he didn't make her feel so helpless. He had this strange effect on her: disabling her mentally and physically, leaving her weak and shivery, as if she had some strange illness.

'*Are* you here alone?' he asked, and she gave him a nervous, frowning look.

'What?' Her lids fell over her aquamarine eyes. 'No, of course not.'

He smiled crookedly, mocking her. 'Who else is here?'

'I told you, my uncle and aunt!'

'Good, I think it's time I talked to them. You said Alex wanted to apologise to me; now is as good a time as any.' He walked towards the open door into the house and she ran after him, in great agitation.

'No, you can't... He's not here... I mean, he's out at the moment; he won't be back until later.'

She was too late to stop him. He was already in the kitchen, looking around him curiously at the copper utensils hanging in neat rows on the dark brown walls, the red and green curtains at the windows, the modern electric stove, the bright green cushions in a basket chair beside the kitchen table.

'Very cosy,' Patrick said, then sniffed. 'Coffee? That smells good; is there any left?'

'No, and you can't stay here!' said Antonia.

He threw himself into the basket chair, and stretched with a sigh of content, like one of the cats she had been feeding, and she felt a strange quiver of reaction deep inside her. His lean, supple body was a pleasure to watch, just as the graceful movements of the cats were good to watch.

She had believed that all her sensuality had been killed that night on the beach, but it hadn't; it was alive now, stirring under her skin as she watched him.

His vivid blue eyes watched her expression, assessing it. There was a fraught little silence; she heard herself breathing, knew her body had quickened, her blood running faster, her heart beating harder.

'How many times do I have to tell you? You don't have to be afraid of me,' Patrick said softly, and she listened to the sound of his English voice and wondered how she had ever managed to mistake that other man's voice for Patrick's. They were quite different.

'I'm not afraid,' she lied.

He looked through lowered lashes at her, smiling mockingly. 'No? Then can I have a cup of that coffee?'

She had trapped herself, left herself open to that. She had to give in, and, sighing, poured him coffee and handed it to him, being careful not to touch his fingers as he took it.

Over the rim of the cup he surveyed her with sardonic amusement, knowing she had avoided touching him. He drank some coffee, then put the cup down. 'Very good. You know how to make coffee the way I like it.'

'Oh, thank you,' she said furiously, hearing that as patronage, and he smiled at her again, crookedly.

'You aren't expecting your uncle back for a couple of days, are you?'

She opened her mouth to lie and met his dry gaze, then fell silent, biting her inner lip.

He gave her a mocking smile. 'Very wise of you not to lie. I rang your uncle's agents and asked where he was, and they told me he was in England for the next few days. Which means that you're in this house alone—which surprised me. I would have thought you'd be nervous of living here alone.'

'Venice is one of the safest cities in the world,' she hurriedly said. 'There is very little crime here. Criminals can't use cars, which means it's hard for them to get away; even if they used a boat they would be spotted at once. I feel very safe here.'

'Even with me around?' he drawled, watching her colour.

She looked down, breathing unsteadily. 'If you've finished your coffee, tell me why you came, and then please go!'

'My landlord just told me he needs my room for his cousin, who has been evicted from his own place, so I have to find somewhere to live pretty quickly. I've started looking around, but Venice is crowded with tourists at the moment, and I can't afford a high rent—I wondered if Alex would rent me a room here just until I find somewhere else.'

She was taken aback, her nerves jumping. 'Oh…well, as I said, he isn't here at the moment, but I don't think he could, anyway. I don't think he would be allowed to sublet a room.'

'And you don't want me here?' Patrick suggested, watching her flush deepen, her sea-blue eyes hurriedly look down, hide behind their pale lids, which had a bluish tinge, too, as if blurred by shadows or frosted by long nights of weeping.

'It's nothing to do with me,' she stammered. 'Uncle Alex is the legal tenant; it's up to him.' But he was right—the very idea sent shivers down her spine—and she had the feeling he could read her reaction with those narrowed, penetrating eyes.

'You still believe me capable of rape, don't you?' he said with a bitterness that made her flinch.

At that moment the phone began to ring and she jumped about a foot in the air, then ran to answer it, very conscious of Patrick watching her.

'Hello? Oh, Cy,' she huskily said, very pink, turning her back so that Patrick could no longer see her face.

'You sound as if you're getting a cold,' said Cy. 'Maybe you've got the beginning of flu? I heard from Aunt Patsy that you were sick yesterday; flu often starts that way. If you have got flu, don't force yourself to go on working; go to bed and stay there.'

'I'm fine,' she said, holding her voice steady by a superhuman effort. 'There's nothing wrong with me.'

'You don't sound fine. Is anything upsetting you? You aren't cross with me because I've had to come back to the States?'

'No, of course not; I understand,' she said quickly, wishing she dared ask him to ring back, or could tell him there was someone there, with her, but she was afraid of the questions he might ask.

She did not want to tell him it was Patrick Ogilvie. Cy knew about what had happened to her two years ago. Before she began working at the *palazzo* he had had her background checked out, and had found out that she had almost been raped in Bordighera.

When he had asked her to marry him, months later, she had been stricken, had felt she had to tell him why she was refusing, and he had stopped her quietly. 'I know, Antonia; I've known from the start,' he had said. 'I understand how you must feel. I know you haven't dated anyone since then, and that you may not be able to face a normal married life for a long time, but that doesn't matter to me. I think we could be very happy together, Antonia.'

Cy was a quiet, kind-hearted man and was honest enough to tell her that he had a low sex drive, which was why he hadn't married before. Business occupied most of his time and attention. Antonia knew he liked her, enjoyed her company, but there had never been any desire in his kisses, no demands she could not face, and he wasn't even in any hurry to name the date for their wedding.

She, in her turn, had agreed to get engaged to him not because she loved him, but because he had offered her a calm future for the first time in two years, and because everyone else had been so delighted—Patsy, Alex and Susan-Jane had all welcomed the news.

'Is everything OK in Boston?' Antonia asked him now.

'Very much so,' Cy said with obvious satisfaction. 'I got a new client—an international company. It means I'll be even busier, but it's exciting. What did you do today? Find anything interesting?'

She told him about her research into the Munnings drawings, and he was immediately alert.

'Put that aside for me; I'd like to see that before we decide whether to sell it or not. It would fit quite nicely into my own collection.'

Cy had inherited the collecting bug from his uncle, but he brought a cool intelligence to bear on it and already knew precisely how he wanted his collection to develop. He had decided to concentrate on nineteenth-century art. It should have occurred to her that the Munnings portfolio would interest him, but she had had other things on her mind.

'Well, I'll let you get to bed early, Antonia,' Cy said. 'Talk to you again soon; goodnight.'

'Goodnight, Cy,' she said, and hung up after he had replaced his phone.

She turned and met Patrick's coolly mocking stare. 'That must have made the transatlantic line red-hot!' he drawled. 'The two of you are hardly Romeo and Juliet, are you? It was more like a business report than a bedtime chat between lovers.' Then, his voice stiletto-sharp, 'Are you, by the way?'

Dazedly she stared. 'Are we what?' Then she picked up what he meant and felt heat burn her face. 'Can't you talk about anything else?'

'You aren't lovers yet, are you? But then I never thought you would be. You're still covered in per-mafrost, and your fiancé doesn't have a blow torch.'

It was somehow the final straw for Antonia. Her temper raced away from her, she hit him round the face, and saw him rock back on his heels, startled and in-credulous, a dark red mark across his cheek.

She couldn't believe she had done it. She stood there, aghast, staring up at him, her sea-blue eyes wild and stormy between dark lashes, her lips parted, quivering, and a second later Patrick had her in his arms and his mouth descended.

Antonia twisted, struggled, feeling her mind cloud, panic rise inside her, suffocating her. She was thrown back two years, was fighting helplessly against a man's insistent body, a silent scream in her head.

As abruptly as it had begun it ended. The compulsion of his mouth lifted from her; Patrick's head came up, his breathing thick and impeded, his face darkly flushed as he looked down at her, groaning as he saw the look on her face.

'God, I'm sorry. I'm so sorry, Antonia, that was un-forgivable. I lost my temper—not that that's any excuse, but when you hit me something blew in my head and the next thing I knew I was grabbing you, but, please believe me, I never intended to hurt you. That was the last thing on my mind!'

White with shock and fear, Antonia put a hand to her mouth, swallowing convulsively.

'I . . . I'm going to be sick . . .'

She broke off and began to run to the stairs, afraid she would throw up before she got to the bathroom.

She only just made it in time, too distraught to think of anything but the agony of what was happening to her heaving body.

A few minutes later she sat on the bathroom floor with her back against the bath, shuddering and sobbing, having got rid of her entire supper, her short blonde hair a tangled web around her white face.

A sound made her head flick round, her eyes wide, hazed with tears. Patrick stood in the doorway, grim-faced.

'Are you OK? Can I get you anything?' His voice sounded different, unfamiliar, a low, harsh noise that made her tense again.

'Just go away,' she whispered. 'And don't come back.'

His features tightened, his mouth a hard white line, his eyes dark. For a moment she thought he was going to come towards her, and shrank; he gave her one long, last, level stare, then he turned and walked away. Nerves leaping like candles in a wind, she heard him go down-stairs, heard the front door open and click shut. He had gone; she was alone. Only then could she slacken, let go, let the full flood of tears break through the dam behind which she had penned them until now.

# CHAPTER FIVE

WHEN Antonia had cried out all her tears she shakily got to her feet and went downstairs to check that the doors, back and front, were locked, then she went back to the bathroom and took a long shower before climbing into bed and putting out the light. She fell asleep sooner than she had expected; the emotional shock of the evening had used up all her energy. Almost as soon as her head hit the pillow she began to drift downwards into a heavy sleep.

The dream began some time later. It always unrolled like an old film one had seen a hundred times before—familiar, inconsequential, nightmarish. She was on the beach under the warm Riviera night sky; there were people there laughing and talking one minute, the next they had gone, just as the moon kept coming and going behind clouds. Even the sound of the sea had a sinister note, a whispering, menacing sound, as she walked in Patrick's footsteps, already half expecting the lunge of terror which came a moment later. He sprang out at her from darkness and she screamed, before the rough hand clamped down over her mouth and she was pulled down on to the sand, struggling uselessly.

It always happened the same way, a deadly routine dulled by time yet still terrifying. She saw a face, tanned skin, bright blue eyes, sun-bleached hair, heard his English voice, thought, It's him; it's Patrick . . . and for a second wavered in uncertainty. Is it a game? Is he playing a joke on me? Her heart beat faster, feeling

Patrick's hands touching her, until she realised the hands were hurting, the body on top of her wasn't playing games. Terror beat back up and she thought as always, Does he think I followed him because I wanted this? A scream formed in her throat, couldn't escape because he had gagged her; and then the worst nightmare of all as he taped her eyes, made her blind, helpless.

This isn't happening, she kept telling herself; it can't be. It's just a nightmare; it isn't real, she thought in her dream, as she had thought that night on the beach. I'll wake up soon, and it won't be true, any of it.

The dream abruptly changed, as they always did, like the spinning of a kaleidoscope, everything suddenly taking on a new pattern. She was still on the beach, but she could see again; the tape across her eyes had gone, her mouth wasn't gagged, nobody was hurting her. She looked up through the windswept tangles of her long blonde hair at Patrick in the moonlight.

'You don't have to be afraid of me, Antonia,' he told her.

'I'm not,' she whispered, but it wasn't true. She was afraid and confused. Had it been a dream, after all? Was she awake now?

'What do you want, Antonia?' Patrick softly asked, then put out a hand and touched her breast, and she saw suddenly that she was naked, and gasped. His fingers trailed across her bare pale skin and she cried out with pleasure and shame.

'Patrick...'

He bent his head and kissed where his hand had lain, and the pierce of desire was like a hot knife.

'No,' she cried out, shuddering. 'Don't...oh, Patrick, don't; I don't want you to do that...'

But she knew she was lying, that she ached to have him touch her like that. It was a tormented confusion between fear and desire that made her deny him and her own feelings, pushing him away. She came up through the cloudy layers of sleep to find herself in her bed, her sheet wound round her like a shroud.

Still dream-dazed, kicking and struggling to break free, she heard movements, the sound of running footsteps, and her nerves leapt with panic. She fought free of the sheet to look at the door, but sat up only to be hit by the solid wall of a man's chest as someone threw himself at the bed.

For a second she was so confused that she didn't know whether she was awake or dreaming, but her senses told her, This isn't a dream; this is real.

Antonia began to scream.

'It's OK, it's only me. You're safe; nobody's going to hurt you,' Patrick hurriedly whispered, pushing her face down into his shirt with one hand clamped behind her head.

For an instant she ached to stay there, buried against him, safe. His body was warm; she heard the deep rhythm of his heart under her cheek; her nostrils inhaled the scent of his skin, a maleness which made her quiver.

But it wasn't safe being that close to this man. It made her want to be closer, and at the same time it made her blood run thickly in panic. She had to get away from him.

She began to struggle, and at once he let her go. Antonia half tumbled back against the pillows, breathing wildly.

Patrick leaned over and switched on the bedside lamp. Dazzled by the sudden explosion of light, Antonia blinked blindly at him, trying to slow her breathing.

When she could control her voice enough she stammered, 'What... what... are you doing here? How did you get back into the house? The doors were locked. I checked them myself.'

'I never left,' he coolly informed her. He was sitting on the side of her bed, still wearing the black shirt and jeans he had been wearing earlier, although they looked a little creased now, as if he might have slept in them.

She breathed audibly, staring while she took that in. 'You mean you hid somewhere?'

His brows met. 'I didn't hide!' he said curtly, offended. 'I went into the sitting-room.'

'There was no light on in there when I went down!'

'I didn't put one on. I sat in the window-seat and looked out into the garden.'

'All this time you've been here, in the house, while I thought you had gone?' She found that thought alarming; her blue eyes dilated, their pupils shiny as black sloes against the pallor of her skin. 'Why did you do that?' she whispered.

He looked angrily at her, his features taut and grim. 'Don't look at me like that! Why the hell do you think I stayed? I was worried about you; you were in such a bad way I was afraid to leave you alone.'

'If I was in a bad way it was your fault!' she threw back at him, and saw his face tighten even more, as if she'd hit him.

'OK,' he muttered reluctantly. 'Maybe I was afraid I might have triggered bad memories, brought it all back——'

'And you felt guilty,' she broke in, and his eyes flashed.

'Until I remembered that you were engaged, and I asked myself what sort of marriage it was going to be if you couldn't even stand being kissed!'

She stiffened, her eyes sliding away sideways. 'But you're not the man I'm going to marry!'

He leaned towards her, and she felt a pulse begin to beat in her neck.

'Then tell me he makes love to you and you like it!'

'I'm not talking about my private life to you!'

'That's just the trouble, though, isn't it? You haven't talked about it to anyone.'

'I saw a therapist back in the States!' she retorted, bristling.

He gave her a disbelieving stare. 'If you did, it didn't help much, or you wouldn't be so screwed up now.'

'I'm not!' She was getting angrier, her eyes brilliant with resentment. 'Just because I don't want you to kiss me doesn't mean I'm screwed up. You may believe that every woman you meet goes weak at the knees at the sight of you, but——'

'I've never had a woman throw up because I kissed her before!' he roughly muttered, his mouth hard, and then he said, 'Just now...you were having a nightmare, weren't you?'

She shot him a look, glanced down, nodding. 'You...heard me?'

'Yes,' he said tersely.

A wave of heat went through her as she remembered what she had been dreaming when she woke up—Patrick's hands caressing her, his mouth on her naked breast, all the drowning sensuality, the piercing desire. Oh, God, she thought, what did I call out? What did he hear?

She looked down, but couldn't help watching him secretly, through her lashes, her face very hot. She was sure she had called out his name, but had she said anything else that might have betrayed what she was dreaming about?

'You were dreaming about that night, weren't you?' Patrick asked in a harsh voice.

She hesitated, then reluctantly nodded.

His face tightened. 'Why did you call out my name?'

'Did I? I can't remember...' She tried to lie, but the words stuck in her throat.

'Don't pretend you didn't!' he muttered. 'I heard you. You yelled my name. Tell me the truth. Did you dream it was me?'

She trembled, her lashes stirring against her cheek, hot colour burning up her face. 'No!'

He put a hand under her chin and pushed her head back, forced her to look at him, his narrowed eyes searching her face, probing for clues in the shifting, confused gleam of her own eyes.

'No? You didn't dream I was the one attacking you?'

She silently shook her head.

He kept looking into her eyes and she was afraid he might read the shameful tangle of desire and fear, the confusion of her reactions to him.

Her eyes slid away and Patrick softly asked, 'Then what was I doing in your dream? Why did you keep saying my name? Why did you say, "Patrick, don't!"? Why, Antonia?'

Desperately she lied. 'I don't know; I don't remember.'

'I think you do,' he said, staring fixedly at her mouth, his eyes dark and intense, and she felt her lips begin to quiver and burn, as if he were kissing them. Her heart was racing; she was breathless.

'Please go away,' she pleaded, her voice a faint whisper.

'Why are you trembling, Antonia?' he asked in that soft, husky voice, and she trembled even more.

'I'm not.'

'Liar,' he said, his mouth curling. He put a long index finger on her throat, and she started violently.

'What are you doing?'

'There's a pulse beating there, at the side of your neck,' he said smokily, his fingertip pressing down into her skin, on the blue vein, and she felt her pulse racing under the touch of his flesh.

'Stop it,' she whispered.

'Is it really that scary?' he asked, and of course it wasn't; that wasn't why she wanted him to stop. She wanted him to stop because she liked it too much.

He ran the finger slowly, inch by tormenting inch, up her throat to her jawline and then to her mouth. Watching her like a cat waiting for a mouse to emerge from a hole, he teasingly drew his finger along her parted, trembling lips, and her breathing almost stopped; she was transfixed, staring up at him, eyes stretched to their utmost.

She could have pushed his hand away. She should have pushed his hand away. She didn't; she just sat there as if hypnotised.

'What did I do in your dream, Antonia?' Patrick whispered, and she was sure he had guessed, or he wouldn't be playing with her like this.

She had a curious sense of unreality, no longer certain whether this was happening or not, whether she was dreaming or not.

His finger slid down from her mouth and trailed silkily downwards again, over her pale throat, to the delicate lace edging her fine, transparent lawn nightdress.

When his finger reached for the white ribbons tying the bodice of her nightdress and she saw him staring at the flurry of lace and lawn and ribbon through which her smooth white breasts could just be glimpsed, she broke out of her trance. Gasping, she pushed his hand away, grabbed the sheet, and pulled it up over her shoulders.

'Get out!' she muttered, looking angrily at him over the top of the sheet. 'And this time, I don't just mean out of this room. Get out of this house! Or do I have to call the police?'

He slowly got up, pushing his hands into the pockets of his jeans, his lean body tense and formidable.

'Have you ever dreamt of your fiancé?' he asked coolly.

'Get out!' she yelled.

'I didn't think you had!' he said, as if she had answered him. 'Try to get some more sleep, Antonia, and be careful what you dream about, won't you? What would you do if your dreams came true?'

She didn't have to react to that. He was already going out of the door; she heard him running down the stairs and climbed hurriedly out of bed, and followed him, meaning to watch from the top of the stairs, making sure he actually left the house.

He paused at the front door and looked back, as if quite aware of her standing there. His blue eyes gleamed like sapphires in the dark and he lifted a hand in mocking salute.

'Did you know that material is totally transparent?'

She leapt back out of sight and he laughed. There was a mirror hanging in the hallway; she watched it and saw his reflected figure leave, the front door slam shut behind him.

Antonia ran down and bolted both front and back doors this time, then methodically searched each room to make sure there was no one in the house except her. It was almost dawn by then; the sky was a milky white, gauzy mist hanging over the Grand Canal, cloaking the outlines of the buildings on the opposite bank, the moorish fretworked stone, rose-pink and dusty cream, the cracked and crumbling plasterwork, the uneven roofs, the cupolas, domes and spires which made up Venice's skyline. They all blurred into a soft composition of line and shade above the rippling, mist-hung water.

Antonia made herself some hot chocolate and went back to bed with it, sat there, brooding in the growing light, remembering his touch, the sensual note in his voice as his finger caressed her throat, her mouth, her breast. She was trembling, shuddering; she was so hot, and her skin prickled with erotic sensation.

She must never, never let herself be caught with him alone again. Not now he knew he could get to her like that.

She got up and showered half an hour later, dressed, and made herself a very early breakfast of fruit and hot rolls from the bakery near by. She might as well go to work. At least she'd be out if Patrick came back.

When she went home the following evening she was on edge as she walked across the sleepy little square towards the pink house in case Patrick Ogilvie had climbed over the garden wall again, and was waiting for her.

Putting the key in the lock, she stiffened, hearing voices inside. Who on earth could that be? There was laughter, the clink of glasses, a slow American drawl. A smile lit her face. Uncle Alex's voice! He was home.

She turned the key, pushed open the gate, looked across the garden and stopped dead, her face blank and shaken. Alex Holtner was there, certainly, lounging on the bench under the fig tree, a glass in his hand. But with him was Patrick Ogilvie.

Casually perching on the edge of the fountain, splashing one hand idly in the water as he talked. His bronzed hair gleamed in the sunlight, and at the sight of him she felt the usual confusion—the stab of attraction, the underswell of fear.

She forced herself to walk into the garden, fighting to look as normal as possible, and both men looked d.

Uncle Alex got up, smiling warmly, and came over to greet her with a kiss and a hug.

'There you are, darling! I wondered when you'd get back. Have you been OK on your own? No problems?'

'None I couldn't handle,' she said, meeting Patrick's mocking blue eyes over his shoulder and coldly looking away again.

'Good girl.'

'Is Susan-Jane in the house? I'll go and find her,' Antonia quickly said, but Uncle Alex shook his head.

'No, she didn't come back with me; she has gone to stay with her cousin Jan in Kent, the one who just had a baby.'

'Why didn't you go too?'

Alex grimaced. 'Oh, Susan-Jane asked me to, but . . . well, Jan is OK but I find her husband Rod a bit heavy going; he seems to think that because I'm a

cartoonist he has to be funny. The trouble is his idea of
humour is a lead balloon. Ten minutes of his company
and I want to hit the guy. So I flew home instead.'

'I'm glad you did,' she said, aware all the time of
Patrick's ironic eyes.

Alex grinned at her. 'Were you lonely without us? Nice
to be missed. I've missed you, too, honey. Sit down and
talk to us. Patrick and I are having a very civilised chat
in the shade—after London it seems so hot here, especially indoors; the garden is the only place I can
breathe. Have a glass of home-made lemonade.'

She had been hoping to escape, think of some excuse
for going into the house, but, with Patrick's derisive gaze
fixed on her, she had to stay. He would only think she
was running away from him.

'Thanks, I'm dying of thirst,' she said, and Alex
Holtner picked up a large deep blue glass jug and poured
some of the contents into a glass, ice chinking as he held
it out to her. There were thin slices of lemon floating on
the surface of the drink, a sparkle of frosted sugar on
the rim of the jug. Antonia's mouth was parched; there
was perspiration running down her back after her walk
back here from the Accademia *vaporetto* stop, not to
mention from the nervous tension of being in Patrick
Ogilvie's company. She took the glass and drank,
thirstily.

'Good?' Uncle Alex said, smiling as she lowered the
glass, more than half empty already.

'Delicious!' she admitted, sitting down on the bench
and fanning herself with the white sun-hat she had been
wearing on her short blonde feathers of hair.

'I gather you and Patrick met at the *vaporetto* stop
at the Accademia the other day,' her uncle said.
'Amazing how that sort of coincidence always seems to

happen. It's a small world. I was just telling him how glad I am to have the chance to say sorry about our mistake in Bordighera—I did write to his publisher, but the letter was returned unopened; I think they had lost your address, Patrick.'

'I moved and didn't tell them,' Patrick coolly said.

Uncle Alex laughed. 'Good for you. I often think I'll do that—move far away, and not tell anyone where I'm going. Especially my publishers.'

He looked at Antonia. 'Patrick has had a piece of bad luck, Tonia. He has had to get out of his lodgings, and is staying in a rather nasty, cheap hotel, so I've invited him to stay with us for a few days. That's OK with you, isn't it, honey?'

Antonia was appalled. Huskily she said, 'But...where would he sleep? There's no room.'

Alex shrugged that aside. 'Oh, he can have the room on the top floor. It isn't very big and it isn't very nicely furnished, but it's not uncomfortable. I showed it to him, and Patrick seemed to think it was satisfactory.'

Desperately she said, 'But are you allowed to sublet part of the house?'

'I'm not asking Patrick to pay; it isn't subletting,' Alex cheerfully said. 'He's just our guest.'

'I'm very grateful,' Patrick said. 'You should see the room I'm living in at the moment. It's like living in a furnished dustbin. It's very kind of you, Alex.'

Antonia was too horrified to risk arguing any more. Her sea-blue eyes stared rigidly up into the black shadows of the fig tree, her hands tightly clasping her glass of lemonade. He had somehow managed to talk his way into the house; he would be staying here, under the same roof! She felt an icy shiver run down her spine. Why was he so determined to push his way into this house, into her life?

Was he still angry because of what happened two years ago? The first time she had seen him again, standing on the deck of the *vaporetto*, she had picked up a black anger in him. It had showed in his face later, as he walked towards her across this garden, having tracked her like a predator and cornered her here. Those blue eyes had glittered with a cold desire to hurt, but he had seemed to change later, to soften, be almost gentle.

He was a deceptive, dangerous opponent. Last night, in her bedroom, he had touched her so seductively.

Her body shuddered now, remembering it. The smooth trail of his finger on her neck, her mouth, still seemed to her to lie there. She had not managed to wash them off when she showered this morning; they had been there all day. Sometimes she had looked into the mirror with bewildered eyes, almost expecting to see their trace; but they had not been visible, she had simply felt them, like the heat of a fire on her skin.

He had marked her, as if she were his territory and he were laying his scent on her to warn off all other males.

She felt him watching her now, and, tormented, wondered if it had been deliberate, if he had intended her to be unable to forget the way he touched her. Did he know that the memory of those moments in her bedroom had been haunting her all day?

What was he up to? What did he really want? She suddenly wondered if she still reminded him of the girl who had changed her mind about marrying him. An odd little pain stabbed inside her. She didn't want to remind him of someone else.

She didn't want him living under the same roof, either. The very idea sent her into a state of terrible panic, but Uncle Alex was so relieved to be able to make it up to Patrick for the way he had been treated at Bordighera that it never occurred to him that she might mind.

Patrick knew, though. He was watching her with glinting, narrowed eyes. If only she knew what he was thinking! Had she been right first time, when she'd seen him on the *vaporetto*, coming towards her with a face like a threat? Did he want revenge for being accused two years ago?

Uncle Alex cheerfully looked at his watch. 'I tell you what, we must celebrate! I'll go and ring a restaurant, book a table for the three of us, for dinner.'

Hurriedly, Antonia burst out, 'Do you mind if I don't come? I'm hot, and tired——'

Uncle Alex laughed. 'Not too tired to eat at La Primavera, I bet? That's Antonia's favourite restaurant, Patrick; she never misses a chance to eat there. I'll go and ring them at once, then I must ring Susan-Jane. She'll be delighted when I tell her I've run into you again and that you're going to stay with us for a while.'

'If she isn't happy with the idea I'll find somewhere else as soon as I can, tell her,' Patrick said, and Alex grinned at him.

'Susan-Jane loves having visitors; she's very hospitable.'

Antonia moved to follow him, and her uncle smiled affectionately at her. 'No, Tonia, you stay out here and enjoy the shade; you're looking very flushed. I won't be long.'

When he had gone Patrick said softly, 'He's right; I noticed you looked very hot and flustered. Is something wrong?'

As if he didn't know very well! 'Look,' she muttered, 'I'm sorry if you can't find anywhere else to stay, but I'd rather you didn't stay here, and I'd have thought you'd realise why!'

'Of course I know why,' he said, and she gave him an incredulous look.

'Then . . . doesn't it bother you that having you under the same roof will keep reminding me of something I've spent two years trying to forget?'

'And have you forgotten it?' he drawled.

She bit her lip. 'No,' she had to admit, then broke out, 'But having you around isn't going to help!'

'How many times do I have to remind you that I wasn't the man who attacked you?' he angrily asked, and she paled.

'I know, but——'

'But as you can't hit back at the man who did, you're determined to make me pay his bill?' he harshly asked, and she was horrified.

'That isn't true!'

'Then why don't you want me to stay here? Do I really look so much like him?' He caught her shoulders, his hard blue eyes hunting over her face. 'Look at me, Antonia. Do I really look like him?'

'I don't remember what he looked like!' she burst out, and saw his face tense, his eyes narrow.

'But you remember me,' he thought aloud in a low, flat voice.

She didn't answer. How could she possibly confess to him that he had been haunting her dreams for two years? She hadn't even realised herself, until now, that she had no idea what the other man had really looked like, although she had never forgotten Patrick.

'Do we have to keep talking about it?' she whispered. 'I'm going up to change.' She began to hurry towards the door, only to find her way barred.

'I wish I knew what went on inside your head,' he said. 'I'm beginning to wonder if you blame me, even though you do realise it wasn't my fault it happened.'

Her eyes widened in shock. 'Of course I don't!' she denied, although she wasn't quite sure she was being strictly truthful. There had been times when she had half blamed him, because if he hadn't forced her to notice him and then walked off she wouldn't have followed him and been attacked.

'You don't hate me?'

'No!'

'Prove it,' Patrick said softly.

Antonia stared at him with bewilderment. 'What?'

'Show me you don't hate me,' he whispered.

He reached down and picked up one of her hands. She stiffened at his touch, and his blue eyes watched her intently.

'If you don't blame me, or hate me, why do you keep jumping every time I'm anywhere near you?'

'I can't help it!'

'Is it so terrifying just to have me hold your hand?' he coaxed, and she bit her lip, then shook her head.

He smiled suddenly and her heart turned over at the charm in that smile—the little lines that creased in that tanned skin beside his eyes, the crook of his mouth.

He lifted her hand and she drew a sharp breath as he held it against his cheek.

Watching her, he turned his head slightly and his lips brushed her hand. Antonia couldn't move, couldn't breathe properly. His mouth opened against her palm; his tongue moved lightly, moistly, and she began to shake

so much that she swayed. At once his arm went round
her waist and she tensed, ready to fight, to run, to push
him away.

'Was that so frightening?' he softly asked, smiling
again, and she slowly relaxed again.

'No, of course not.' She tried to back away, her eyes
flickering nervously. 'Alex will be back any minute.'

'What a tiny waist you've got,' Patrick said, his hand
pressing along her spine, pushing her closer, closer, until
there was barely any space at all between them.

She put her hands against his shoulders to thrust him
away, shivering. 'Stop it! Let go!'

He relaxed his hold again, but didn't let her go. Staring
down into her eyes, he murmured, 'What was it you
didn't want me to do in your dreams, Antonia?'

Hot colour rushed up her face; her sea-blue eyes
widened like great pools of stricken light.

'Was it this?' Patrick asked, and his mouth swooped,
moving urgently, hotly, against her parted, quivering lips,
his tongue-tip sliding between them.

For a second she just stood there like a stone statue,
then she fell back into darkness again, back in the confusing, disturbing dreams that had haunted her for two
years. She was torn between a wild attraction and a sick
dread, fighting herself as much as him, not even sure
who he was now that her eyes were shut and he was just
a male body touching her, intimately, sending these
tremors of devastating upheaval right through her,
making her want him, even while she hated him.

She had been too young to learn how desire felt before
that night in Bordighera, when all her natural instincts
were dammed up at once. Since then, she had refused
to let anyone close enough to get through to her. Now

the dam had broken and the flood waters had burst through; she was shuddering with wild erotic feeling.

And then another, even more disturbing thought leapt out at her. If she had not been attracted to Patrick Ogilvie, if she had not followed him down to that beach, she would never have been attacked.

The panic came surging back; she began to fight, gasping, sobbing, a blind terror in her face.

Patrick stopped kissing her, and raised his head, frowning down at her, then caught her shoulders and shook her. 'Stop it! Stop it, Antonia!'

She looked at him wildly, a sob in her throat as she whispered, 'Let go of me, then!'

He didn't; he put both arms around her and held her even closer, pushing her head down on to his chest. 'Ssh, calm down; stop fighting me,' he murmured, beginning to stroke her hair, his hand light, moving rhythmically.

The violent tremors running through her body slowed gradually until they stopped. She leaned on him, her breath catching for another moment, and then her breathing grew regular again; she gave a long sigh.

Patrick pushed her backwards, lowered her on to the bench, and sat down next to her, leaving space between them. He looked levelly at her. 'OK, now, tell me about it. Why did you go into hyper-panic suddenly? And be honest with yourself, Antonia. What really scared you just now?'

She looked down at the dark pattern of the fig leaves moving on the gravel.

'Isn't it obvious?'

'Not really. One minute you were kissing me back——'

'No! I didn't!' she broke out hoarsely.

He seized her chin, turned her face towards him, tilting her head up so that she had to look into his set, stern face. 'Antonia, we both know you were. Do you really think I can't tell whether or not the woman in my arms wants me to make love to her?'

Heat blazed in her face; her sea-blue eyes filled with shame and misery. 'I didn't! That's a lie! Don't say that!' She felt tears welling up, trickling down her face, and saw Patrick's face darken, tighten into a stiff, formal mask.

There was a silence, then he said quietly, 'You're terrified of admitting it, aren't you?'

She sobbed, put her hands over her face.

Another pause, then Patrick produced a clean handkerchief and began wiping her face, drying her eyes. 'Stop crying, Antonia. Come on, cheer up before your uncle comes back and blows a fuse when he sees you looking like a cloudburst.' He handed her the handkerchief. 'Here, blow your nose.'

She obediently blew her nose, while Patrick got up and walked away, prowling around the sunny garden, his hands in his pockets and an abstracted frown on his face. She didn't look at him, yet she picked up his mood, and wished she knew what he was thinking.

She fished her make-up case out of her bag and with a shaky hand did something to repair the damage to her face, made herself look normal, just as her uncle came out of the house, smiling.

'Well, Susan-Jane says the baby is gorgeous, but she's missing us already and will be back soon. She sends her love, Tonia.' Then he turned to grin at Patrick. 'And guess who she ran into in a street in Colchester? Rae Dunhill.'

Patrick looked startled. 'Rae? What on earth was she doing in Colchester?'

'Apparently she's doing a book on the Boadicea uprising against the Romans, and it seems Colchester was the first place they burned to the ground. I'm not even sure where Colchester is—except that it's in Essex and Susan-Jane is staying near there with Jan and her husband. There are lots of Roman remains to be seen, however; and Rae is there, doing research.'

'She's always very thorough,' Patrick said, grimacing. 'Who's doing her illustrations now, I wonder?'

'She's been doing them herself,' Alex said. 'But she told Susan-Jane she badly missed having you to work with; she says the books you two worked on together are selling like hot cakes and the illustrations have made a big impact.'

Patrick smiled. 'Well, that's good news—I've only earned small advances so far; it will be nice to get some more money from them.'

'Susan-Jane is having dinner with Rae tonight,' said Alex. 'It occurred to me...to us...that maybe you might be interested in working with her again? What do you think? If she flew back with Susan-Jane would you talk to her, Patrick?'

Antonia watched Patrick, jealousy stabbing at her. But she had no right to care whether or not he started working with Rae Dunhill. She was engaged to another man.

He sat there, on the edge of the fountain, his long legs crossed, swinging one shoe and staring at it as if it fascinated him. His face was intent, jawline rigid, mouth a hard line.

'Well?' pressed Alex Holtner, watching him too. 'If you're interested, next time I talk to my wife I'll tell

Susan-Jane to invite Rae, then the two of you can take it from there.'

Patrick slowly looked up, his mouth twisting drily. 'Do that, Alex. I was in a very bad mood last time I saw her, but I've got over that now.'

'Terrific!' Alex grinned.

'Well, I've regretted walking out on my deal with Rae ever since I did it, and I'd like a second chance with her,' shrugged Patrick.

Antonia drew a sharp breath. Exactly what did he mean by that? Just that he would like to work with Rae again? Or that he would like a second chance with Rae in a more personal sense? Antonia wouldn't have been surprised to be told Rae was in love with him; there had been something very possessive in the way she talked about him, and Rae was a very attractive woman. But how did Patrick feel about Rae?

'Let's go to dinner,' Alex said, smiling broadly.

It was a strange evening. Alex and Patrick did most of the talking; Antonia said very little but she listened intently, especially to Patrick. Every so often he would look at her small oval face, the sea-blue eyes, which watched him so intently in the candlelight, and then she would look away, the soft fair curls falling over her temples like stray feathers.

She couldn't help wishing she had never seen Patrick on the *vaporetto* the other day. Ever since, he had been complicating her life; and she had had enough of complications, didn't think she could bear any more.

It got worse over the next few days. She began to feel as if she was coming apart at the edges, fraying day by day, unravelling helplessly.

They met at breakfast every day with Alex and talked as they sat around a table out in the garden with the early morning light playing over their faces. Rolls with black cherry jam and coffee had never tasted so good, and she lingered over them for too long and had to rush to get to the *palazzo* on time.

Sometimes, later on in the day, she went to the Accademia to research an uncatalogued painting in the *palazzo*, or ask advice from one of the experts who worked there, and usually Patrick was working there too, and they would walk back to the house together in the late afternoon, through echoing quiet squares, along narrow winding alleys, over bridges, talking about High Venetian art, the miraculous skills with which Renaissance painters mixed and made their own paints, talking of oils and tempera and techniques used by favourite artists like Michelangelo or Donatello.

Patrick was far in advance of her, both in the theory of art and in practice, as she realised from watching him draw or paint, awed by his ability. She was learning as much from him as she ever had from one of her teachers.

In the evenings the three of them went out to restaurants or stayed at home in the little pink house to eat spaghetti cooked by Alex, a salad made up by Antonia, or a risotto Patrick had invented, full of seafood and herbs.

After their meal they listened to music and played cards; often Alex went out to visit a friend and Antonia and Patrick were left alone, talking in the garden as the light drained out of the sky and the warm Venetian night began.

Antonia knew what was happening was dangerous, but she felt more alive when she was with him. When she wasn't with him she thought about him all the time, and her moods became changeable, unpredictable.

For months she had been going along quietly, leading a calm, safe, uneventful life. Now, suddenly, she felt as if she were on a fairground switchback, whirling through gaiety, excitement, alarm, aching uncertainty, at every turn, and all because of Patrick Ogilvie.

Two years ago she had done him a grievous wrong. She knew that. She had felt guilty ever since. Well, now Patrick was getting his own back, knowingly or otherwise. Because of him she was wildly happy one minute, miserable the next, and she didn't understand why; she only knew that Patrick was the cause of all her odd moods.

# CHAPTER SIX

THERE was a sudden heatwave the following weekend. The soft autumnal mists which had hung over Venice blew away on Thursday night, and next morning the sun was blazing as if it were July again. Antonia was so hot that she had to move slowly at work that day. Patsy told her to go home after lunch, which they had together.

'See you on Monday; I'm off to have a siesta. Why don't you do the same, darling, when you get home?' she said, lethargically fanning herself with a real nineteenth-century Venetian fan made of black silk and lace, sprayed with hand-painted red roses, as she made for the stairs.

On her way home, Antonia decided Patsy was right; it was too hot to do anything. She would go straight upstairs to her room and lie down with the shutters closed to keep the heat of the day out. When she got back to the little pink house, though, she found Patrick sitting in the garden, sketching, under the fig tree.

'You're early,' he said, glancing at her sideways as she tried to slip into the house without his noticing her arrival.

She halted, shyly said, 'Hi, isn't this some heatwave? Patsy sent me home; she said it was too hot to work.'

'She's right; I was just going to stop. Come and see this. What do you think? Have I managed to get those shadows on the wall right?'

She stood behind his shoulder and stared at his pen-cilled sketch of the house. 'It's terrific,' she said, admiring his technique. He was better than her by miles; he always would be. She wished she had his talent.

He put his head back to look up at her, his face oddly inverted, the lids half down over glimmering blue eyes, smiling. 'Thank you.'

She felt a tremor deep inside her, and turned away, her breath catching. 'Well, I'm going to have a siesta for an hour or two.'

'Come to the beach instead,' he said, standing up. 'A swim will help cool you down and afterwards you can sleep under an umbrella.'

'The Lido will be too crowded today.'

'Not by the time we get there.' He looked at his watch. 'It's gone three now; it will be half-past four before we get on to the beach. Come on, this is the perfect weather for the Lido.'

She looked up at the deep blue bowl of the sky, cloudless and brazen. He was right; this was a day for being on the beach. She had a sudden yearning to plunge into the sea, feel cold water breaking over her whole body. She looked at Patrick's coaxing face and gave in, shrugging.

'OK.'

The Lido of Venice had originally been a barrier of silt built up over centuries by local rivers rushing down from the Dolomite mountains, carrying mud and sand which was thrown out into the Adriatic and stuck there, forming a very elongated, narrow island with some fine sandy beaches which became the playground of Venice. Always crowded, these were now lined with cabins, some belonging to the Lido's grand hotels, others rented by local people or visitors.

Antonia hadn't often been over there, but she had stayed at the Grand Hotel des Bains for a few days once.

One of the gracious, faintly old-fashioned hotels from
the nineteenth century, the hotel had a private beach near
by, and Antonia could remember spending hours there.

Today, though, Patrick took her to another beach,
where they each rented a mattress and umbrella, side by
side. The beach wasn't as crowded as she had thought
it would be, since the heat of the day was subsiding now
and people were beginning to leave the beach and head
for home, but there were plenty of people still around—
children running about, laughing and shouting, teenagers
splashing in the sea, playing beach-ball, and older people
asleep in the shade.

Antonia was wearing a smooth-fitting black swimsuit
which left her tanned shoulders, arms and legs bare, but
demurely covered the rest of her. When she emerged from
the changing-room to find Patrick waiting she was very
self-conscious, expecting some teasing comment from
him, but apart from flicking a wry, narrowed glance over
her he merely said, 'Do you want a long, cool drink
first, or shall we have a swim right away?'

'A swim,' she said, dying to get into the water.

'OK,' Patrick agreed, and they both headed for the
water's edge, the hot sand burning the soles of their feet.

Antonia only meant to splash around a little, to get
cool, but while she was idly swimming along Patrick
suddenly dived beside her and she felt him grabbing her
feet and pulling her under the blue lagoon.

She gave a little scream, half laughter, half alarm, and
kicked violently, forcing her way back up to the surface,
and began to swim far faster.

'You can't get away from me, Antonia!' he called out,
and she felt her heart knock at her breast.

She put on a further spurt, using all her energy to
push herself through the water. She was quite a good

swimmer, and she was very fit. Without thinking, she headed out further and further from the Lido until the sounds of voices, the laughter and chatter, died away behind her and the only sounds she heard were the slap and splash of the waves around her, the laboured breathing of her own lungs, and the sound of Patrick forging a path behind her.

He reached for her again and she put on another burst of speed to get away.

'Antonia, what the hell do you think you're doing?' he yelled, but she ignored him, her eyes almost closed as water swirled across her face while she swam onwards.

She was tiring now; her body seemed very heavy, it was hurting to breathe and her muscles were aching. How much longer could she go on? she thought. Maybe she should head back now?

Getting worried, she slowed, shot a look over her shoulder, and saw Patrick's set, grim face not far behind, his bronzed hair dark with sea water, his arms and shoulders smoothly working to push him through the waves, and far, far behind him the beach in the distance, hazy in the late afternoon sunlight, the figures of people on the sand seeming very small, and wavering, like mirages.

It was further than she had thought it would be. She bit her lip, beginning to turn, and that was the moment when cramp struck. A spasm of pain hit her and she gave a cry of agony, corkscrewing, beginning to sink, struggling. She had never felt pain like it.

As she cried out she swallowed water and began to cough and choke, going into panic as she realised she was in serious trouble.

Patrick reached her a moment later. 'What's the matter?'

'Cramp. Terrible cramp,' she breathlessly groaned.

He gave her a furious look; she expected him to shout at her, but instead he lifted his head clear of the water and looked around, groaning. 'And we're a hell of a long way from land.' Then he stiffened, staring to one side for an instant, before quickly turning back to Antonia. 'Look, if you can't swim, could you float, do you think? I've just seen a small sand bar over to the left. If we can make it there you can rest for a while until you're fit enough to swim back to land. Will you risk it? You'll have to trust me. If you start panicking, we could both drown.'

The cramp was getting worse; she was in such pain that she could barely stand it. She nodded, unable to speak. Patrick gave her a searching look, frowning.

'OK, put your arms round my waist, and go limp; float on the top of the water if you can and try to keep to one side of me, so that I can use my arms and legs to propel us both along.'

She shakily obeyed, sliding her arms around the middle of his body, and fought to ignore the cramp still torturing her. Patrick began to swim, pulling her along with him. She felt every movement of his body as it drove through the water, his legs rippling along beside hers, his body cold and wet in her arms. It wasn't easy to stay limp, to give herself up to his control. Fear thickened her throat, she was shivering violently, and the minutes seemed to drag by. The cramp in her legs seemed to be getting worse; she had to bite on her lip to stop a cry of anguish.

At last, though, the waves threw them both up on the narrow sand bar, like drowned animals. They lay on their faces, panting, trembling; it was several minutes before

Antonia could even sit up and start massaging her cramped legs, feeling the agony gradually subside.

Patrick sat up beside her a moment later, his chest still heaving and his breathing noisy.

Antonia gasped out, 'Thank you; you saved my life.'

'It's always stupid to take risks with the sea,' Patrick said, looking sideways at her, his hair slicked down against his skull, making the strength of his bone-structure stand out.

'I realise I was stupid,' she said crossly. 'No need to rub it in!'

'I just want to be sure you won't do that again; I might not be here next time,' he said drily. 'How's the cramp now?'

'Better, thanks.'

'Well, we'll have a rest before we head back to shore,' he said, and lay down full-length on the fine sand, his long body lazily relaxed. 'Mmm... that sun is wonderful. I don't know about you, but I'm chilled to the marrow after being in the sea that long.'

'I'm very cold,' she agreed, watching him. He had his eyes shut, which made her feel safe enough to risk staring. He was almost naked, the tiny black briefs he wore clinging wetly to his body, revealing more than they concealed. She hurriedly looked up at his face, afraid he might catch her staring, but his eyes were still closed. Breathing more easily, she let her gaze wander back to his wide, tanned shoulders, that strong chest with the dark, wet tangles of hair which ran down his flat stomach and on until they disappeared under the waistband of the close-fitting briefs. No denying it, Antonia thought, dry-mouthed. He has a sexy body. Staring at his powerful thighs and those long, long legs, she felt heat begin to burn inside her.

The slow rhythm of his breathing altered at that second—quickened, was far more audible.

Antonia shot a tense, startled look at his face and was horrified to find Patrick's eyes wide open. He had been watching her while she looked at him, she realised in shock, and a second later he reached out and caught her waist, jerked her downwards so that she fell on top of him. The impact of their bodies hitting each other sent her lungs into hyper-drive; she couldn't get a word out for a minute.

'Kiss me, Antonia,' he whispered, his eyes very blue in the Venetian sunlight.

She shook her head wordlessly, deeply conscious of his body touching hers so intimately.

He murmured, 'You won't lay your ghosts until you've admitted you have a body and it has very physical instincts, Antonia.' His fingers twined themselves into her wet hair. 'Don't be scared; just let those instincts take over. Kiss me.'

'I can't,' she groaned, but she couldn't stop staring at his mouth.

It smiled at her, a warm and passionate curve. 'Yes, you can, if you stop telling yourself there's something wrong with wanting to.'

'Who says I want to?' She pretended indignation, very aware of his blue eyes staring up at her intently, as if he was trying to see inside her head. She was afraid he could, too; she was afraid Patrick was telepathic, could read her every thought, every feeling.

Why was she so vulnerable to him? How did he make her feel this way? Why this man, rather than any other? Right from the moment she first saw him she had felt like this about him.

He kept staring into her eyes and his deep, low voice tormented her. 'Kiss me, Antonia.'

'I don't want to,' she lied.

'Yes, you do,' Patrick said, and he was right; she did. She was dying to kiss him, and at the same time scared to death. But how did he *know* that?

'Antonia, how can you talk about getting married when you freeze every time a man comes within a foot of you?' he asked.

'If you know I'm so scared, why are you always trying to make me kiss you?'

'You aren't scared of me, Antonia. That isn't fear you're feeling, is it? Do I really have to tell you what it is?'

She gave him a distraught, flickering look. 'Stop talking like that!'

'If you don't want me to talk about it, stop me talking,' he whispered. 'Kiss me.'

'Well, if it's the only way to shut you up!' she said crossly, took a deep breath, and swooped down at him, brushed her mouth over his, a light, butterfly kiss gone almost as soon as it touched him.

'Now can we swim back to the beach?' she said, unsteadily.

Patrick didn't answer; he had closed his eyes; his tongue-tip moved along his mouth. Antonia watched, dry-mouthed, unbearably excited.

'You taste of the sea,' he said softly. 'Let me taste you again.'

She bit her lip, staring at the parted curve of that sexy mouth, her heart beating heavily, wanting to kiss him so much that it was an agony. She couldn't bear it—she had to feel his mouth again; she slowly lowered her head. As her mouth touched him she felt his tongue move softly between his lips to meet her, and an involuntary groan broke out of her.

'Patrick,' she moaned, deaf to her own voice, her eyes shut tight, letting herself sink into the dark bliss of sensuality for the first time in her life.

After that night in Bordighera she had felt for a while as if she were in a dodgem car, crashing around helplessly, being knocked from here to there by life without having any power to dictate her own direction. She had been terrified by the instability, the uncertainty that that night on the beach had revealed to her. That was why she had accepted Cy's proposal. He had offered her a calm, secure life with a man she liked, who would never hurt her or frighten her.

She had felt threatened again ever since Patrick came back into her life. She had never forgotten him, even though she had only seen him so briefly at that party in her uncle's house two years ago. The attraction had been immediate, devastating; and, ever since they'd met again, that feeling had intensified hour by hour, day by day: the deep beat of a dangerous drum, a growing excitement, which might explode at any second and blow her life apart.

She felt that drumbeat now, her whole body shaking as Patrick deliberately moved against her, the damp-furred masculinity of his inner thigh brushing against her, making her shudder with erotic sensuality. His hands moved too, tormenting and caressing, making her whimper with aroused desire, with frustrated need.

Her ears beat with the rhythm of her own blood; she was deafened by her heart thudding, blind to the glitter of the sun, the blue sea, the blue sky. All her senses were wrapped up in Patrick, her responses to him, a growing pleasure which was more intense than anything she had ever known.

When Patrick suddenly caught her shoulders and pushed her upwards, holding her away from him, she was dazed and confused, her eyes opening, staring down at him in bewilderment.

'We'd better get back to the beach; this sun is far too hot,' Patrick huskily said, his face darkly flushed and his blue eyes moving restlessly.

Antonia barely heard what he said. She was watching his mouth move and was hardly able to breathe. Everything in her was concentrated on that one point in the universe—Patrick's mouth. She could have looked at it for hours without growing tired, but most of all she wanted to kiss it again; she could spend eternity kissing his mouth.

Patrick said roughly, 'I didn't expect to get this far this fast. If we stay here any longer I can't guarantee things won't go even further.'

Her face burned.

He gave her a dark, smouldering look. 'I don't want to be accused later of using force, or making you do anything you don't want to do, so from now on you're going to have to ask for it if you want it, Antonia.'

Her breath caught as if he'd hit her. 'You do think a hell of a lot of yourself, don't you?' she threw back at him, and then scrambled to her feet, dived in without a second look at him, and began swimming, heard him splash into the sea a moment later.

Her cramp had gone, but she was still very tired, and was relieved to get back to the beach. She collapsed on to her mattress, put on her headphones, and, ignoring Patrick as he joined her, listened to a new tape of one of her favourite groups while she drowsed and sunbathed. By that time of the afternoon the sun was low in the sky, shadows were lengthening, people were leaving the beach, yet the air was still languorously warm and the sky was still blue.

Antonia slid into a light sleep, began to dream of Patrick kissing her; she woke up, turning on to her side in restless agitation, to find him lying next to her, watching her with those half-closed, tormenting eyes.

Her skin began to burn. No wonder he knew what she was thinking, when he kept eavesdropping on her dreams. When he did that, he was invading her most secret space, her own mind, her unconscious, the place to which even she did not have all the keys.

'Stop watching me!' she angrily burst out.

'You were asleep; why should it bother you?'

'I'm awake now!'

'Sure about that?' His eyes were full of laughter, but she was not amused.

'Very funny. You may enjoy playing games; but I don't.'

'You don't know how, that's all,' he softly said. 'You need a few lessons on how to enjoy life.'

'Not from you!' she snapped, turned her back on him again, switching on her cassette player and turning up the volume to drown out anything else he said.

They got back to the little pink house just as the sun was sinking, and found a note from Alex telling them to eat without him.

Bumped into an old chum and having dinner with him and his latest wife! May be late!

Antonia nervously flicked a glance at Patrick. 'Well, maybe we should eat out tonight, too?'

'Ten minutes ago you said you were too tired to move,' he reminded her drily. 'Look, you have a shower; I'll cook supper.'

'Not spaghetti again?' she ruefully asked, and he made a face at her.

'My spaghetti is world-famous. But no, I shall cook something new and exciting. Go on, woman, have your shower, and leave me to my mysteries.'

She reluctantly went up to her bedroom, locked the door, stripped, took a lukewarm shower, and put on a thin blue and white striped cotton shirt and white jeans.

When she got downstairs again there was a delicious scent coming from the kitchen, but Patrick shouted out, 'Lay the table, will you?' so she got the cutlery out of a drawer and began to lay the table for two. There was an opened bottle of red wine on the table already, and a woven basket of sliced bread, so she put out two wine glasses and lit the candles in the green bronze candlesticks standing in the centre of the table.

'Ready,' Patrick shouted, and came in from the kitchen carrying in one hand a large flat terracotta dish which he placed in the centre of the table.

'What is this?' She could see that the main ingredient was some sort of scrambled eggs but mixed up with sliced green and red peppers, onions, ham and tomatoes. 'Is it an omelette that went wrong?'

'Certainly not; my cooking doesn't go wrong. No, this is *piperade*, it's a Basque dish. Haven't you eaten it before?'

She shook her head. 'I'm not sure I'd like it.'

'So you keep saying,' he said with soft mockery, and watched her crossly flush at the double meaning, the sexual teasing.

'I don't think you're funny!'

'I know you don't. Come on, Antonia, try it; I know you're going to love it.'

He was right; it was delicious, as was the wine, and the music on the compact disc player. While they ate, Patrick talked about the great Venetian artist, Tintoretto, whose painting was a mixture of mystical fantasy and soft, subaqueous Venetian light. Antonia listened, watching the candle-flame smoke and twist in the night breeze from an open window.

When they cleared the table and washed up, Patrick began sketching her. Dreamily she sat in the candlelight, watched herself grow under his deft fingers: a slender creature with dishevelled light curls and drowsy, languorous eyes, a girl with her own familiar features, yet someone startlingly different, a new self, invented by Patrick.

He pushed the sketch over to her later. 'Well, what do you think?'

She looked at the mouth of the girl in the sketch; parted and sensuous, it wasn't hers. Nor were the glimmering, inviting eyes.

'That isn't me,' she said huskily.

Patrick got up and unhooked a small Venetian mirror from the wall near by and propped it up in front of her, on the table. 'Look at yourself,' he said in a low, slurred voice, leaning over her shoulder, his face against hers. 'It is you, Antonia, as you should be, not as you think you are.'

She looked, her senses drowning, and couldn't deny it—the reflection exactly matched the sketch, the girl with her aching, parted mouth, the eyes full of sensual, erotic yearning.

'The first time I saw you, you looked like that,' Patrick said, and she gave him an angry, jealous look.

'The first time you saw me, your engagement had just been broken off, and you were in no mood to find me sexy!'

He grimaced. 'I was angry that night; I'd been angry for days,' he admitted. 'But I couldn't take my eyes off you from the minute I saw you. When I heard, afterwards, what happened later that night, I felt as guilty as if I'd done it, because I knew I had wanted you myself.'

'That wasn't the impression I got!'

'No,' he said grimly. 'I wish to God I had gone over to you, danced with you, even taken you to bed—if I had you wouldn't have been on that beach alone, would you?'

Tears pricked her eyes. She got up, stumbled to the door, and ran upstairs without saying goodnight.

She was awake half the night imagining what might have happened two years ago if Patrick hadn't slapped her down and walked off. If he had danced with her, as he'd said, taken her to bed.

Would I have gone? she asked her brooding triangular cat's face in the mirror of her dressing-table, her elbows propped on the bed facing it.

Yes. Oh, yes. That night, that moment, like ripe fruit falling off a tree, she had fallen for Patrick. She hated to admit it, but she couldn't deny the truth any longer. If he had reached out he could have taken her easily, because she had fallen in love with him at first sight; but he hadn't reached out, he had walked away, and two years of her life had been blighted.

Sometimes I think I hate him, she thought, looking into her slanting, angry eyes in the mirror. I'd like to make him suffer the way he did me. I'd like to see him on his knees. If he gives me that mocking, sexy smile once more and tells me to ask for what I want, I'll scream!

She turned over and buried her hot face in the cool pillow, but that only reminded her of his mouth, the feel of it under her own, the taste of it. Groaning, she turned on to her side again. It was a very long night, but by dawn she had finally fallen asleep. At least she didn't have a nightmare that night.

Over breakfast, Patrick told her and Alex that he was going out across the lagoon to the island of Murano, where he was having glass-blowing lessons with a friend who had a workshop over there and was a famous glass-maker.

'Why don't you come, Antonia? You could take a lesson yourself; you might well find you have a flair for working with glass. You have strong wrists and a good eye.'

She knew it was a beautiful trip out across the misty reaches of the lagoon on a fine summer morning, but she found the prospect of making that journey with Patrick far too disturbing after last night.

'Thanks, but I have other things to do,' she said coolly.

Patrick gave her a dark, smouldering look, but in front of her uncle had to accept the answer.

She spent the rest of the day imagining what it would have been like to go with him, see the opalescent mists rise as the *vaporetto* sped over the water, and the sun came through, to stare up at the cemetery island of San Michele, the white walls, behind which were white Carrara marble monuments, the tall, dark flames of cypresses burning against the blue sky, the angels, flowers, and photographs of the dead on the graves. The whole island had a melancholy tranquillity, which she loved.

She knew, by now, that Patrick's passion for such places matched her own. They had found out so much about each other from their hours of talking about painting, sculpture, music, perhaps even more from the silences that fell now and then when both of them sat watching the light on the falling spray of water from the fountain, the dark shadows of the fig tree shifting on the gravel, the sound of pigeons cooing on a warm afternoon.

She went for a walk along the *riva* for an hour that afternoon, and when she got back the front door was opened by Susan-Jane.

'I didn't know you were coming today!' Antonia said, delightedly hugging her.

'I was missing Alex; don't tell him!' Susan-Jane grinned at her. 'You're looking very well, I'm pleased to see. How's Cy? Is he back?'

Self-consciously, Antonia shook her head. 'Did Rae Dunhill come with you?'

'She's upstairs, unpacking,' said Susan-Jane. 'I'd better go and help. Could you make us all a long, cool drink?'

Antonia went to mix drinks, listening to the others upstairs, unpacking, filling the little pink house with laughter, perfume and the sound of talking. Wardrobe doors clicked open, hangers rattled, drawers slammed shut, voices called from room to room, and downstairs Antonia listened edgily.

'I have to be in Florence next Tuesday,' said Rae Dunhill.

'But you'll stay until then?' asked Alex.

'If you can put up with me that long!'

The Holtners laughed. 'Of course we can! We wouldn't have invited you if we hadn't wanted you! And you and

Patrick will have plenty of time to talk and get your plans settled.'

Rae laughed softly, huskily. 'Oh, I can't wait to see him again! We work together so well; he was always able to make my ideas visual; and that's not something I could say about any other artist I've ever worked with. I hope he's back to normal now. He was an absolute pet to work with until Laura Grainger broke off their engagement.'

Antonia wished she knew what Laura Grainger had really been like. Patrick rarely mentioned her name. Everyone said she looked like Laura Grainger, but Rae had said Laura was beautiful, and Antonia knew that *she* wasn't. She was too thin, had no figure and no sex appeal, and, for the last two years, she hadn't wanted to have any.

'Laura can't possibly have found anyone better than Patrick,' Rae said upstairs. 'I hope you're right, Alex, and he's his old self again!'

'I'm not sure what his old self was like,' Alex said drily.

'He was a lamb,' Rae said. 'I was always able to manage Patrick, get him to do what I wanted.'

Antonia didn't believe a word of it.

Susan-Jane sounded surprised, too. 'He doesn't seem the biddable type. In fact I'd have said he was quite a difficult guy.'

'He never used to be!' said Rae. 'Patrick wasn't one of your male chauvinists; he wasn't the type to throw his weight around or expect to be boss in a relationship with a woman.'

'Are you sure you're talking about the Patrick Ogilvie we know?' Susan-Jane said laughingly.

'I don't suppose you know him very well yet,' Rae said complacently. 'Patrick likes strong women. Laura Grainger was one, you know—very tough, very ambitious. And Patrick was absolutely crazy about her.'

Antonia felt a painful clutch at her heart, and her eyes opened in shocked self-realisation. She was sick with jealousy, couldn't bear to think of Patrick being 'crazy' over someone else.

'I'd heard she was gorgeous to look at, and very clever,' said Susan-Jane with open curiosity. 'I wonder why she dumped Patrick and married someone else. What had the other guy got that Patrick hadn't?'

'I rather gathered he was a farmer somewhere remote in England, still living in the Dark Ages as far as relations with women were concerned. I'd have hated him. Patrick and I always worked well together because he let me make all the decisions!' Rae Dunhill laughed, yet under her amusement was quite serious.

Susan-Jane said drily, 'You wouldn't like working with Alex, then—he wouldn't let you make his decisions for him!'

'Sorry, Rae, but she's right!' Alex said, sounding even drier. 'I'll cook a meal for Susan-Jane if she's tired, look after her if she's ill, and when we have to make plans together we discuss them and come to some mutual agreement, but I won't let her make all the decisions, any more than I'd expect her to let me make them. We share everything fifty-fifty.'

At that moment Antonia heard Patrick arriving back. He walked into the kitchen and she felt her heart beating so fast that she was afraid he might actually hear it. Suntanned, slim, in well-washed blue jeans and a white T-shirt, his brown hair bleached to a gleaming bronze, he took her breath away; she couldn't bear the idea of him with Rae. She looked at him with jealousy and pain, and Patrick stared back at her, his brows pulling together.

'Don't look so delighted to see me, will you?'

'Rae and Susan-Jane have arrived,' Antonia said flatly.

His face changed. 'They have?' He turned, listening to the sound of voices upstairs, and smiled. 'I thought they were coming on Monday!'

'They managed to get an earlier flight.' Antonia watched the sunlight gleam on his brown skin, the line of jaw and mouth, the strong throat rising out of the T-shirt, which clung like a second skin to his body. He was so sexy; desire ached inside her, and she swallowed.

The voices were approaching; Susan-Jane and Alex were talking, interrupting each other happily, telling Rae Dunhill some long anecdote about Venice. A moment later they all walked into the room and Rae stopped in her tracks, holding out both hands, a smile lighting her face.

'Patrick!'

'It's good to see you again, Rae!' he said, taking her hands and looking down at her, smiling back.

Antonia watched with intensity, noting every expression, every tone of voice, the vibes between them making her nerves jangle. She wished she knew exactly how Patrick felt about Rae; that he liked her was only too apparent. But precisely how did he like her? As a friend? Or was there more than that in it? He had worked with Rae long before his engagement was broken off. Had his relationship with Rae had anything to do with the ending of that engagement? Had Laura Grainger been jealous of Rae? Antonia wished she knew the answers to all the questions buzzing around her head.

Alex Holtner said cheerfully, 'Let's all go out to celebrate. Do you have a favourite restaurant here, Rae?
Or will you let us choose?'

Rae broke off her eager chatting with Patrick to look
round. 'Actually, I do have a favourite place—Antico
Martini——'

'It's ours too! When we feel rich enough to afford it,'
Susan-Jane interrupted, laughing.

'I'm paying,' Rae promptly said.

'Oh . . . no . . . I didn't mean . . . that wasn't a hint, just
a joke! Of course we're paying!' Susan-Jane said, going
pink with embarrassment.

'Next time you can pay, and choose where we go,'
said Rae. 'But let me foot the bill this time, a little thank-
you for inviting me here!' She smiled in a friendly way,
but Antonia, watching her, saw that under the fine
delicacy of her features there was great strength in her
face, an insistence and certainty that she must get her
own way.

Rae Dunhill was a strong woman. Was she the sort
of woman Patrick wanted?

'Oh, well, then, thank you,' Susan-Jane said, grace-
fully shrugging. 'But at this late hour I doubt if we can
get a table.'

Alex Holtner walked over to the phone. 'We can soon
find out. I'll ring and ask if they have a table for five.'

'Four,' Antonia quickly said, and everyone looked at
her. 'I promised to be in this evening; Cy is ringing from
the States.'

'Oh, what a pity,' Rae Dunhill said politely. 'I was
looking forward to getting to know you better.'

'He could always ring again later,' Patrick curtly said.

'Yes, but I have a headache, too,' Antonia lied. 'It's
been so hot here for the last few days.'

'Yes, it is sultry weather.' Rae Dunhill came to her rescue, but that didn't make Antonia like her any better. 'It was raining in London when we left. You are looking rather pale, you poor girl—maybe you had better go to bed?'

'I think I will; Cy won't ring for another hour or so,' Antonia said, avoiding meeting the stiletto probe of Patrick's stare. 'I hope you all have a lovely evening.'

In her room she undressed and put on a blue-striped satin nightshirt, then sat on her bed, doing her nails, and listening to music to drown the sound of voices and laughter downstairs. She didn't want to hear Patrick sounding so happy or Rae Dunhill sounding triumphant.

She heard them leave, but they didn't get back until nearly two. It was a suffocatingly hot night, and she was wide awake, her nerves stretched to breaking-point. Alex and Susan-Jane came upstairs at once, but it was another hour before the other two made their way to bed.

Antonia heard Patrick's voice—warm, intimate, murmuring something she didn't catch—heard Rae laugh softly. Stairs creaked as someone made their way to the top floor. Alone? wondered Antonia, and rolled on to her front, buried her face in her pillow. She did not want to hear them talking to each other, nor anything else they might do together.

Over the days that followed she managed to stay at the *palazzo* as much as possible, so that she saw very little of Rae Dunhill, and even less of Patrick.

That the two of them had come to an agreement, that Patrick was to work with Rae on her books again, she did know, from Uncle Alex, who was very pleased about the outcome of his manipulation.

'You see, all they needed was to be brought together! They were both being stubborn and proud; they wouldn't get together of their own accord. They make a perfect pair, though; they suit each other down to the ground. I'm glad I managed to make them see sense.'

A few days later, Rae moved out of the pink house and moved on to Florence again. She left very early one morning, before anybody else was up, except Antonia, who was in the kitchen getting herself some coffee and fruit when Rae walked in with her case.

'I'm just off, Antonia,' Rae said, watching her peel a peach, and Antonia gave her a startled look, not having been aware that Rae was leaving so soon.

'There's plenty of coffee and some fresh rolls which I just got from the bakery round the corner,' she offered, but Rae shook her head.

'No, thanks, I'll get something at the airport. I said goodbye to everyone else last night; I'm sorry I haven't seen more of you while I was here, but you must come and stay with me in Florence some time.'

'Thank you,' Antonia said in cool courtesy. 'Have a safe trip.'

'Give Patrick my love when he gets up,' Rae said, smiling.

Over my dead body! thought Antonia. What she actually said was, 'I thought he might go back to Florence with you?'

'I wanted him to, but he says he has some unfinished business here, in Venice; and I couldn't get him to change his mind.' Rae frowned impatiently. 'Just between you and me, Patrick has changed more than I'd expected. He used to be easy to handle, but he's become difficult. In fact, I'm not so sure we're going to work together as well as we did. We can't both have our own way, and this is my project we'll be working on!'

Antonia couldn't think of anything to say to that, except a fatuous, 'Oh, dear!'

Rae gave her a dry glance. 'Yes, well, I mustn't bore you with my problems—I'd better be off. See you around, no doubt. I'm glad to hear you're engaged, and have got over what happened at Bordighera.'

Antonia didn't have to answer; even if she had wanted to she wouldn't have been able to interrupt Rae's quick, crisp tones as she walked to the back door and into the garden, carrying her luggage in both hands. She would walk to the landing-stage, where a water taxi would take her to the airport.

'Goodbye, my love to everyone,' Rae said, and Antonia echoed her.

'Goodbye.'

Uncle Alex came down a moment later, having been woken by the bang of the door closing. Antonia told him Rae had left.

'Yes,' he yawned indifferently, 'she said she was leaving early, to catch the Florence plane. A very efficient lady, that; she ordered her own taxi, made all her own arrangements. A rather taxing guest to have, though; she expects the best, and no doubt gets it most of the time.'

'I thought Patrick would go with her, Uncle Alex. How much longer is he staying?'

Alex shrugged. 'Until we leave ourselves. I told him he could stay as long as we were renting the house. Rae has negotiated a new agreement for him with her publisher, and he hopes to be able to afford a much better apartment here once the advance comes through.'

'He's staying on in Venice?' Antonia's voice wasn't quite steady. Her feelings were as changeable and contradictory as April weather. For the past few days she had been miserable because she'd believed he was going away with Rae, and now she was on edge at the prospect of him staying on in Venice.

'For some time,' Uncle Alex said casually, seeming not to notice the way her colour fluctuated, the constant changes in her mood.

Antonia hesitantly asked, 'But I thought he was going to be working with Rae Dunhill. How will they manage that if they live in different cities?'

'They talk on the phone and she sends him her type-scripts by post. They don't need to meet all that often, after all.'

Alex and Susan-Jane were leaving, too, in a few days. Antonia was moving out of the pink house into the *palazzo*, at Patsy Devvon's invitation.

She had been given a little suite of rooms of her own in a quiet corner of the enormous, rambling building, much to Lucia's deep resentment. But Antonia was de-pressed about leaving the pink house. It was such a tranquil, enchanting little place, with its walled garden and fig tree, the pigeons which cooed and strutted on the roof in the evenings, the dusty silence of the square beyond the gate.

Antonia knew she would never forget it. It was where she had first realised she was in love with Patrick, and memories of him were now closely, inextricably en-twined with memories of this house. She had so many images of him here to remember—Patrick lounging by the fountain, splashing the water with one hand while he talked, Patrick feeding the pigeons with the crumbs from his breakfast rolls, or watching her under the dark shadow of the fig tree, his blue eyes like summer lightning in the sunny air.

For two years a dark vision of Patrick had haunted her sleep, fed her nightmares, made her heart beat agonisingly. These weeks in Venice had given her other visions of him to set against that—yet they had not cancelled each other out. Patrick still frightened her, still obsessed her dreams. The guilt of knowing that she had followed him down to that beach because she wanted him was a scar on her mind. How could she forget that if she hadn't followed him she would never have been attacked?

She had fallen in love, and that same night she had gone down into hell, believing with horror that the man hurting her was the man she had fallen in love with at first sight. Even finding out that it hadn't been Patrick hadn't been able to unravel the confusion of her heart, the disturbing threads of passion and fear, of desire and repulsion, which had been entangled inside her ever since.

The last week at the pink house was very busy. While Alex and Susan-Jane were packing up all their belongings, Antonia packed her own things, and then Patrick helped her take the cases down to the quayside, where a water taxi was waiting to carry them all to the *palazzo*, which, of course, had its own landing-stage.

Although she said she could manage, Patrick insisted on coming with her, his curt manner making it impossible for her to argue in front of the amused and watchful boatman.

'Get in!' Patrick coolly ordered, taking her by the waist and lifting her down into the boat. It infuriated Antonia that this high-handed treatment should meet with grinning approval from the boatman.

Patrick dropped down into the boat too, said to her, 'Sit here!' took her shoulders, and pushed her down into a seat, as if she were a child.

A moment later, the launch set off across the canal. Antonia crossly stared out at the blue sky, the exquisite

backcloth of Venice edging the water on each side, the
golden mosaic and cupolas of San Marco falling into
the distance, the bend in the Grand Canal speeding
towards them, shimmering with pink and cream *palazzi*,
fantasies in stone, the embodiment of the Serenissima,
the serene republic of Venice.

They docked at the *palazzo*; Patrick helped her move
her cases inside, into the inner courtyard, filled with
terracotta pots of orange trees and roses, with geraniums and tumbling ivy and ferns clinging to the walls,
making a green shade in which one could sit on a hot
summer day. From the courtyard one climbed the stone
stairs to the main floor, to the *portico*, a long, gloomy
room more like a wide corridor, but lined with wonderful paintings and sculptures, with tables displaying
some of the Devvon collection. The *portico* ran from
the front of the building to the back, with rooms opening
off on each side.

Lucia met them there. '*Madame* is out having coffee
with the *baronessa*. You know where your room is!' She
eyed Patrick forbiddingly. 'And who is this man? Why
are you bringing strange men in here without permission
from *madame*?'

Antonia explained who he was; Patrick kissed Lucia's
hand, and to Antonia's amazement a little pink flush
crept into the woman's olive skin.

'A painter, is he? I know what they're like, even more
wicked than men usually are!' she bridled. 'Well, I'll
make some coffee for you while you're carrying the bags
upstairs.'

'He isn't staying; I can manage,' Antonia said crossly,
resenting the way Patrick had so easily wound Lucia
around his little finger.

'You aren't carrying all this upstairs!' Patrick curtly told her, picking up most of the cases and beginning the long climb up the ancient marble stairs.

'I can see you don't find him as easy to deal with as *madame*'s nephew!' Lucia cackled, her black eyes watching Antonia with witch-like amusement.

Antonia picked up the small cases Patrick had left for her to carry and went after him, her face very flushed.

He was waiting for her at the start of another long, shadowy corridor room with doors opening off in all directions. 'Which room is yours?'

She walked ahead to the high, dark, varnished door of the suite, which stood open, went inside, and put down what she was carrying. Patrick followed, put down her cases, and looked around the sitting-room in which they stood, then gave a long whistle of disbelief. 'This is magnificent. What a huge room. But there's no bed.'

'That's next door; I have a whole suite.' She was childishly rather pleased to tell him that, but if she had expected to impress him she was disappointed.

Patrick gave her a steady look, and walked off to explore the other rooms in the suite. Antonia followed him, watching the vivid blue eyes flick everywhere with that sharp, perceptive gaze, but unable to tell what he was thinking.

'So this is the palace your absentee fiancé is going to inherit one day!' he drawled, turning at last, his brows lifted derisively.

She nodded warily, knowing he was going to make some biting comment.

'I can see why you find him so attractive!'

The insult sent the blood rushing to her head. 'That's a vile thing to say! I'm not interested in Cy's money;

that's not why I'm going to marry him! I would marry him if he hadn't a penny in the world!'

Patrick's blue eyes watched her flushed, angry face remorselessly. 'So long as he didn't try to make love to you?'

That was too close to the truth to be bearable. She hit out blindly, but Patrick was too quick for her. As her hand came up he caught her wrist and pulled her roughly towards him.

'You weren't going to hit me, were you, Antonia? Careful, you're starting to lose control, and that would never do, would it? You have to keep your natural impulses on a very tight rein or you might betray the fact that you're a woman with all a woman's instincts and needs.'

'Let go of me!'

'In a minute,' he said softly. 'But first...'

The kiss that took her mouth was so powerful that it forced her head back, made her instinctively clutch at him to stop herself falling over. His mouth was hot and relentless, making it hard to breathe let alone talk. She resisted feverishly, feeling like a straw swirling into the centre of a maelstrom, helpless to break free and dizzy with the pull of the tide dragging her deeper.

He let go of her hands, but only to draw her closer with one arm around her waist. She could have broken away then, but his mouth held her like a magnet; she quivered, drawn irresistibly to that tender north, her own mouth parting, yielding to the passion of his kiss.

She felt his hand moving, moulding her body, like a sculptor making a figure out of formless clay, firmly following the angles and curves, possessively shaping her, exploring her, learning her, his fingers warm and sensitive. She began to ache for closer contact, for his hands on her naked flesh; she was shaking, moaning with closed eyes, her fingers curling into his shirt with helpless excitement.

The aroused sensuality of her blood began to beat under her skin, through her veins, around her body, following everywhere his hands went. She was only wearing a brief, sleeveless top ending at the midriff; he pushed it up and unclipped her lacy bra to cup her breasts with his hands, his fingers stroking and caressing.

Antonia was aching to touch him as intimately; she shakily began to pull his shirt open, feeling the heat of his skin through the thin material, and then, at last, slid her hands inside, finding the firm, muscled flesh, the smooth brown shoulders, the flat stomach, her fingers twisting in the short, goldy brown hair which ran down his body.

Patrick was breathing raggedly, a groan of pleasure in his throat; he slid his mouth down her neck, kissing her feverishly.

Their bodies were breast to breast, hip to hip, thigh to thigh; every movement was igniting wild sparks of desire inside her. She shifted restlessly; her hand crept round his neck, caught strands of his hair; she groaned, her thigh moving instinctively against his in explicit invitation.

Patrick broke off the kiss, darkly flushed. He looked down at her, his eyes dark with passion. 'Now, maybe, you'll admit the truth! You aren't in love with Cy Devvon; you've never wanted him like this, have you? If you marry him, you'll ruin his life, as well as your own!'

Antonia stared up at him, stricken, realising that it was true.

# CHAPTER SEVEN

CY RANG Antonia that evening, after dinner, at the *palazzo*, to check that her move had gone smoothly. His aunt had gone out for dinner; Antonia had eaten alone, and was in her room, already in bed. 'I hope I didn't wake you,' Cy said, sounding anxious. 'Has moving exhausted you?'

'It was tiring; I thought I'd go to bed early,' she said, and went on over-brightly to tell him that she had already unpacked her cases, put away her clothes, and had settled comfortably into her new home. All the time she talked, though, she was trying to think of some way of telling him what was really on her mind, but it seemed impossible to raise the subject out of the blue, on the telephone. She wished he weren't so far away; she wished he were here, so that she could see him face to face, but wouldn't that be even harder? Oh, she wished she weren't such a coward.

Her voice must have betrayed her, because when she stopped talking in her husky, uneasy voice a brief silence followed, then Cy asked, 'Is something wrong, Tonia?'

She gave a sigh, half nervous, half relieved. 'Oh, you're so quick! I don't know how you guessed; you must be telepathic. But you're right. Cy, I've been thinking...wondering... Oh, I'm sorry, Cy, I don't know how to put it into words; I'm too confused about everything.'

'Are you trying to tell me you're having doubts about our engagement, Tonia?' he asked quietly, and she gave another long, quivering sigh.

'Yes. Cy, I'm sorry. I don't want to ruin your life, and I'm afraid I would if we got married, because I don't think I'm anywhere near ready for marriage. I should never have said yes; I think I wasn't thinking straight when you asked me.' She paused, swallowing unhappily.

Cy's voice was careful, gentle. 'We can put off the date for as long as you like, you know. There's no hurry, no need for you to feel panicked.'

She bit her lip, knowing she had not told him the entire truth. What she had said was only a part of the truth. Oh, why was she such a coward?

She was afraid to admit to Patrick that she loved him, afraid to tell Cy that that was the real reason why she must not marry him. Ever since that night in Bordighera she had been too scared of life to take any risks.

When she was silent, Cy said on a sigh, 'Of course, I've sensed some sort of change in you since I've been back in the States, I should never have left you over there while I came home. I thought it would make it easier for you to adjust to the idea of marriage if we spent some time apart, but obviously I was wrong. It was a mistake.'

'No, you were right,' she quickly said. 'I needed time to think.'

'You mean, you've spent too much time alone,' Cy drily said. 'Fretting, over what happened to you in Bordighera, and over the future. I know how hard it must be for you, but you've got to put the past behind you and get on with living.'

'I know,' Antonia said in a quiet little voice. 'I've realised that.'

'I only wish I could fly back to Venice today, to talk this out with you,' Cy said impatiently. 'The trouble is, I have a lot on my plate this week. I couldn't spare the time. Look, I'll try to get to Venice as soon as possible, so that we can talk. In the meantime, stop worrying, Antonia. Just live each day as it comes, don't spend too much time alone, try to get out more, and forget about getting married for the moment. I don't want you under any pressure. Take your ring off, if that helps, but lock it in the safe in the *palazzo*, Tonia; don't lose it, will you?' He laughed as he said that, yet she knew he was really serious, because, after all, the ring was worth many thousands of pounds.

'Of course not,' she quickly said.

'Good girl.' He always talked to her as if she were a child and he were the adult in charge of her; why hadn't she noticed that? His indulgent manner, his gentleness, was the way one treated a beloved child. Was that how he thought of her? Well, there was a huge gap in their ages, she thought, really grasping for the first time how much older than her he was. He wasn't much younger than her father, in fact.

Why else had she always felt so safe with him? But why did Cy want to marry someone he saw as a child?

Indulgently, he said, 'We'll talk this out, darling; just relax and trust me. Now get some sleep; you'll feel much better in the morning, I expect.'

After he had rung off Antonia lay in bed, staring at the ceiling, listening to the soft lapping of the water outside, along the wooden piles supporting the *palazzo*'s landing-stage, the sound of the gondolas skimming along the Grand Canal. Her heart was heavy. Cy had not taken her seriously.

No, she thought. I wasn't honest enough with him. I didn't tell him what was really on my mind. Now he thinks I'm just having an attack of pre-marital nerves because of what happened two years ago. But it isn't just that. He doesn't know I've met Patrick again.

She turned over heavily, feeling feverish, restless, confused. She should have told Cy the truth, told him she was in love with Patrick and could never marry him now.

At least she could be sure she wasn't going to break Cy's heart. She was quite certain Cy wasn't in love with her. He had never given her any evidence of passion. His kisses had been soft, kind, gentle. Nothing like the kisses Patrick gave her.

She buried her face in her pillow, her skin burning. She wouldn't think about that now. She must get some sleep, and if she started remembering Patrick making love to her she would be awake all night.

Next day she returned for the last time to the little pink house in the sunny, dusty, drowsing square on the Dorsoduro. Alex and Susan-Jane had packed up all their possessions and seen them dispatched in a van to Monte Carlo, where they would be stored for a few days until their owners arrived to move back into their Monte Carlo home.

That evening, Alex and Susan-Jane were having a party for their friends on their final day in Venice, and Antonia was kept busy most of the afternoon helping them get the house ready, cleaning and polishing, moving furniture around to clear the rooms for a large influx of people, preparing food, chopping and washing salad, and making a variety of easy-to-eat dishes which could be pre-cooked and re-heated, like paella, quiches, pizzas and curried chicken.

When everything was ready they all slumped into chairs and sipped some white wine before they went up to have baths and dress.

'It's so crazy, having a party the night before we leave!' Susan-Jane chuckled. 'We're going to feel like death tomorrow, and we have that long drive ahead of us.'

'But we won't have to clear up here, because I've got a local cleaning sevice coming in to deal with the house!' Alex pointed out. 'And we don't have to drive all the way to Monte Carlo; we can stop if we feel tired and book in at a hotel on the way for a night. Relax, darling; there's no problem we can't solve.'

'You just love having parties!' his wife accused, making a laughing face at him.

'Guilty!' he complacently admitted. 'So do you!'

'We should have had this one a week ago, though!'

'Oh, that just means an anticlimax, knowing you've got another week before you actually leave! No, the best time to have a party is the night before you leave. Then you get up and go!'

Susan-Jane finished her wine and looked at her watch. 'Me first for the bath!' She got up and shot towards the stairs and Alex got up too and lunged after her, but she was too quick for him and vanished upstairs, laughing. Alex came back and sat down, grinning at Antonia.

'She always has to be first in the bath! That gives her more time to get dressed, and she does love to dawdle over dressing for a party; she changes her mind half a dozen times over what dress to wear, what make-up, how to do her hair and so on! You'd think she was deciding the fate of nations, the time she takes to make up her mind.'

'The end product is worth it, though,' Antonia said warmly. 'She always looks gorgeous!'

'That she does.' Alex grinned at her. 'So do you. What are you going to wear tonight? Something wild and sexy or something elegant and sophisticated?'

She gave him a wry look, knowing that neither description ever fitted her. The last thing she wanted to do was look wild or sexy. She preferred not to attract male attention in that way; it was far too risky.

What she had been doing for the last two years was melting into the background as much as possible, trying to be invisible, especially to men. As for elegance or sophistication, much as she admired both qualities in other women, she had never fooled herself that she possessed either. She wasn't the type, neither tall enough nor with the right cool manner.

'I brought my carnival dress, actually,' she said, and Alex Holtner's face lit up.

'That one! I'd forgotten it—you almost never wear it; but you must, tonight. It's wonderful! Nobody will be able to take their eyes off you.'

'Off my costume, you mean!' she drily said, knowing the effect it always had.

It was a dress Alex had bought her here in Venice, not long after they'd arrived. It had been in a sale at half-price, having been designed to be worn for the Venice Carnival, which took place in the dark weeks of late February, when the city was half empty, grey, chilly and wet. The wild explosion of the carnival lit the cold streets for a week, bringing in tourists at the dead season of the year, and thousands of art students from all over Italy, and, indeed, Europe, who came to enjoy the fun and make pocket-money by doing body-painting in the streets for other students who weren't able to do it themselves. The most extraordinary designs were worn around Venice that week—young people in hand-painted masks, wearing 'body' costumes like pale second skins, which were then painted with wild zigzags of colour—orange and gold and black and scarlet—making them look like alien life forms. On really cold days they wore a warm cape which flew around them as they walked, leaving their body-painting visible to passers-by.

Alex Holtner, his wife and Antonia had just missed the carnival, arriving a couple of weeks later, but carnival masks and costumes had still been around in the shops at reduced prices, and Antonia had stopped in her tracks as she'd passed a shop not far from the Rialto market and seen a silver and black dress taking up the whole of the shop window.

Although it was half-price, it was still far too expensive for her, and she would have walked on, but Alex and Susan-Jane had seen the glow of delight in her face, the coveting expression.

They had exchanged a glance, then Susan-Jane had urged her, 'Go in and try it on!'

She had demurred, laughing, shaking her head, but Susan-Jane had firmly led her into the shop and asked to have the dress taken out of the window so that she could try it on. The owner had looked Antonia up and down, with a thoughtful expression.

'Yes, it will fit her, I think,' she had said, and Antonia had been carefully helped into the costume in a cubicle. Seeing herself in a mirror had stunned her. She had gone out to show Alex and Susan-Jane, who had gazed, silenced.

'But I really can't afford it!' she told them sadly, aching to own the lovely thing.

'We can, though; it's our present to you,' Susan-Jane had said, smiling, and Alex had nodded, smiling too. 'You look enchanting in it. It was made for you.'

She had been over the moon. It was a typical generous gesture from them both; they were the most warm-hearted and giving people in the world, and she felt she had been very lucky to have them for relatives. Their love had more than made up for the indifference her parents had shown her all her life.

She had only worn the dress once so far, but it had made the sensation she had known it would. People had stared open-mouthed, had spontaneously burst into applause at the ball she had attended not long afterwards with Alex and Susan-Jane. The dress was meant for some such occasion—a ball, a costume party, a carnival. It wasn't a dress you could wear every day; it was far too striking and fragile. It was intended for very special occasions, and with care would last her for years.

She smiled at her uncle, her eyes misty. 'Oh, I'm going to miss you both! Venice is going to seem empty once you've gone.'

'We're only a few hours away,' he said gently. 'Call us if you need us, any time; you know we'll come. But you're going to love living in the *palazzo*; your suite sounds fabulous, and you're fond of Patsy Devvon, aren't you? When does Cy get back?'

She looked down, her lashes falling against her cheek, biting her lip as she tried to think of the words to explain, to tell him that she wasn't going to marry Cy after all, that she meant to break off her engagement, but then Susan-Jane called out from the top of the stairs.

'Alex! Alex, come and scrub my back!'

He laughed, getting up. 'I'm coming, darling!' he called and lightly ran up the stairs.

Antonia was the last to have a bath and dress, and she took her time, knowing that the party wouldn't begin until nine o'clock and that everything was ready; there was nothing much to do now.

She was painting her toenails silver when Susan-Jane called through the door. 'We're just popping out to buy some more drink; Alex doesn't think we're going to have enough. We just got a call from Pietro to say he's bringing half a dozen musicians with him to give us an impromptu concert in the garden, and you know what musicians are!'

'OK,' Antonia said, contemplating her shimmering toes. She was going to be wearing delicate, thin-strapped silver sandals, and now her toes would match. She began painting her fingernails too.

'Be back in half an hour or so!' Susan-Jane said and clattered down the stairs.

When her nails were all dry Antonia picked up the face mask lying on her bed and tried it on in front of the mirror. It fitted over her nose, covering only the upper half of her face, leaving her mouth, cheeks and jawline bare, an exquisite confection of silvery feathers slanting upwards around the almond-shape of her sea-blue eyes, which looked misty and mysterious between the feathers.

It wasn't easy to get the mask to sit perfectly; she struggled with the strings for several minutes, getting them tangled up in her short blonde hair as she tried to

fit them into place. It was with relief that she heard footsteps on the stairs. Susan-Jane couldn't have left yet.

'Before you go, could you help me with this,
Susan-Jane?' she called out and the door-handle turned.

In the mirror she looked at the opening door with a
smile, watching for Susan-Jane's reaction to the mask,
which Susan-Jane had coveted ever since Antonia bought
the costume.

But it wasn't her aunt standing in the door. It was
Patrick. He was staring fixedly at her; she heard him
inhale sharply and her nerves jangled; wild pulses started
up all over her body.

'Get out of my room!' she burst out.

'You invited me in!' His voice was low, and his blue
eyes had turned a strange, smoky blue as they explored
her reflection in the mirror.

She had not yet put on her dress; she was only wearing
a thin black silk and lace slip which lay on her pale golden
skin like shadows, leaving far too much of her bare.

'I thought you were Susan-Jane. You knew I did; I
called her name! You had no business walking into my
bedroom,' Antonia angrily said. 'Will you please get
out—or do I have to start screaming for help?'

'There's nobody downstairs; I wouldn't bother,' he
said, wandering towards her in a cool stroll that made
her even more edgy. He was wearing a black evening suit
with a tight-fitting waistcoat over a white silk shirt and
black tie. The clothes made him look taller than ever,
his lean body intensely watchable, as graceful as a wild
cat, broad-shouldered, slim-waisted, those long, slim legs
supple and elegant in movement, the evening sunlight
falling like a caress on the strong angles of his face, il-
luminating the blue of his eyes, his tanned skin smooth,

his hair bleached to a dark gold by the sun. Antonia felt waves of emotion sweeping through her: aching desire followed at once by shock, by terrified panic which made her want to run and not look back.

She looked desperately around for her robe, but she had left it on a chair and to get it would have to walk past him.

Calmly he asked, 'Where are Alex and his wife? I thought the party began at eight, and it's past that now.'

'They should be back any minute—they went to get something,' she admitted, then almost desperately said, 'Will you get out of here?'

'Have you any idea how sexy you look?' Patrick huskily murmured. 'There's always been something other-worldly about you—that distance you try to keep between yourself and any man who might try to come too close. But tonight you're glittering, a mythical creature from fairy-tale, half-bird, half-woman.'

She froze, tranced by a vibration in his voice, a low, throaty sound, like the purr of a leopard.

He slowly put out a hand, delicately brushed the soft, downy silver-white feathers. 'What sort of feathers are they? A dove's? Not quite the right shade, though, for a dove; not white, more silver.'

'We were told they were from a silver pheasant,' she whispered.

'Beautiful,' Patrick said, his fingertips running down over the feathers to the filigree silver edge of the mask where it fitted over her cheekbones.

She quivered as she felt his fingers touching her warm skin, slipping downwards to her mouth, following the curve of it caressingly, sending a shudder of arousal through her entire body.

She was hypnotised, watching him through her mask, unable to move an inch, while inside her the successive waves came and went, desire making her shudder, fear making her stomach turn over.

'If you were a bird, I'd want to catch you and put you in a cage,' Patrick murmured. 'If you were a woman, I'd lock myself in here with you, and make love to you for days.' His smile was mocking, but his eyes had that dark, smoky heat in them, and she began to breathe very rapidly, her glossy black pupils dilating.

She tried pretending it was a joke, forced a shaky little laugh. 'You have a weird sense of humour; I don't think that's funny!'

'I wasn't being funny,' he said, suddenly catching hold of her arms and swivelling her round to face the mirror again. Patrick stood behind her, his chin on her shoulder, his hands sliding round her waist and cupping her lace-covered breasts, their soft fullness nesting in his warm palms. 'Are you a woman, or aren't you? Isn't it time you made up your mind?'

'Don't!' she groaned, trying to wrench herself away, but at once his arm tightened on her waist, pulled her backwards; his hard male body forced against her, making her very aware that he was aroused; his thigh pushed alongside hers. The contact completed the electrical circuit flowing between them, the power of his body throbbing along her veins, shocking her, weakening her.

'Stop fighting, Antonia,' he muttered, his mouth pressed down into her throat, his teeth gently grazing her skin. 'Just relax and feel it.'

As if she didn't feel it! She moved restlessly, so conscious of his body pressing into her that she shuddered with a tangled mix of pain and pleasure, the ebb and flow of those conflicting emotions turning her body into a battleground.

'I can't bear it! Please . . . don't, Patrick, I can't,' she muttered, closing her eyes.

'Don't shut your eyes!' Patrick fiercely said. 'Don't try to ignore it; look into the mirror, Antonia! Come on, open your eyes, and take an honest look at what scares you so much you keep running away from it!'

She shook her head, keeping her lids down, her heart hurting inside her.

'If you keep on shutting your eyes and pretending it isn't happening you'll never face up to it!' His voice was harsh now; she felt the anger beating inside him and shivered.

'Don't be angry with me,' she pleaded. 'He was angry, that other man . . . I hate it when you're in a rage; it reminds me.'

'Everything about me reminds you, doesn't it? How do you think I feel about that? When you look at me sometimes your eyes cloud over and I see you shiver and I know what you're thinking about, and I feel like hunting for that bastard and killing him!'

Her eyes flew open and she looked at him in the mirror, sea-blue gaze startled, wide, searching.

Patrick stared back into them. 'Antonia, do you want to be maimed all your life? Sooner or later you're going to have to admit you're a woman, and you need love, and there's nothing wrong or shameful in needing it; it's the most natural thing in the world.' He put his cheek against her own, rubbing his skin on hers, rocking her gently like a child, his arms around her. 'I need it, too. We all do. Human beings need love like plants need rain. You had a bad experience, but if you're ever going to be a whole, natural woman you're going to have to put it all behind you and risk loving again.'

Antonia stared fixedly, saw them both in the mirror, intimately entwined, so close they might have been one, her body pulled back tightly against Patrick's. Her fine, semi-transparent black silk slip hid very little. She was shocked to realise how much of her body was visible to him. She would have closed her eyes again, but Patrick's gaze magnetised her; he refused to let her look away a second time. Holding her gaze, he deliberately began to explore her body. His lips lightly moved against her neck, her collarbone, her shoulder, the mothy kisses making her quiver with pleasure; meanwhile his hands were busy, too, one pulling down the straps of her slip, and then her bra, leaving her breasts naked, softly caressing the firm, pale flesh, the hardened pink nipple. She helplessly watched, trembling, breathing hoarsely, and Patrick watched her face while his hands were wandering, read her reactions.

'There's nothing terrifying about this, is there?' he whispered, her earlobe softly held between his teeth, his words breathed warmly into her ear. 'It isn't scaring you; I'm not hurting you. You like it. Don't pretend you don't. You want me to touch you.'

She couldn't find the breath to deny it, even if she had wanted to; she was having difficulty breathing at all.

'You want me to touch you,' he repeated huskily. 'Like this...' And he ran a hand tenderly down the feminine curve of her body, following her hipline, the warmth of his palm through the thin silk giving her intense pleasure.

'And like this...' he muttered as his hand found the hem of her slip, pushed the deep lace upwards, and slid underneath, stroking her warm, smooth inner thighs.

He had gone too far. She went rigid. 'No! Don't; don't——'

'Don't panic, Antonia; don't start fighting again. It's OK to admit what you want, how you feel,' he softly said, and tears sprang into her eyes. She was so hot that she was burning up; she was violently shuddering, because she had stopped him too late. He knew now that she wanted him; he had found out her secret, discovered the moistness and heat which betrayed her, and was softly arousing it, his fingertip rhythmic, tormenting.

'Oh, no,' she moaned, closing her eyes, stricken and shamed.

He kissed her neck. 'Yes,' he whispered, while his hands went on torturing her with a pleasure that was driving her out of her mind.

Her heart was beating raggedly; she was barely able to breathe, wanting him so much that it was more than she could bear, and yet at the same time still afraid, the shadowy third who was always with them making it impossible for her to give way to her feelings.

'I can't!' she cried out, and Patrick made an angry noise, spun her round to face him, looked down at her, and caught her face between his hands.

'You don't still confuse me with him? What can I do to prove that I'd never hurt a woman that way? I've never in my life had to force a woman to give me what I wanted——'

Antonia gave a sharp little gasp of pain and he stopped talking, and looked down at her, his blue eyes narrowing, searching.

'Was that jealousy, Antonia?' he huskily asked.

She couldn't meet his eyes.

He tipped her head back, a finger underneath her chin, made her look at him, his smile crooked, triumphant. 'There's no need to be jealous; I'd never confuse you with anybody else, darling,' he whispered, making her stomach turn over with tenderness.

Nobody had ever called her darling in that way before. The word made her melt. Patrick bent to kiss her and she instinctively moved to meet his mouth, her lips parting hungrily. In a wild rush of passion she flung her arms around him and moved closer, her hands restlessly touching his nape, his hair, the firm, muscled power of his back.

Patrick groaned, and lifted her bodily off the floor, her feet in mid-air; then suddenly she felt herself falling, weightless, confused. She landed on the bed with Patrick on top of her, and stiffened, her body arched to resist him, a cry of panic in her throat.

'Don't be scared, darling,' he said quickly. 'Don't tense up again; there's nothing to be frightened of; it's me... Look at me, darling...'

She looked at him, wildly, met his blue eyes in confusion and flickering uncertainty, then a long sigh broke out of her. 'Patrick...'

He smiled at her, his blue eyes passionate. 'Yes, it's Patrick, and you don't need to be scared any more. You're not going to get hurt; you know you can trust me,' he said, and kissed her, his mouth warm, reassuring. Antonia kissed him back, beginning to enjoy the weight of his body, the closeness. She wound her arms around him and moved restlessly, her heart beating very fast.

Patrick kicked his shoes off, still kissing her, began tearing his clothes off too, and she feverishly helped, unbuttoning his waistcoat, then his shirt, pulling them both off, her breathing thick and impeded.

She wasn't frightened any more. She was driven by other feelings, other needs. She was finally touching him the way she had always wanted to, from the moment she first had seen him. Desire had flowered so instantly, so hotly, when she looked at him that what happened a short time later had been like a hard frost on new buds, blackening and freezing them. She had thought her desire killed. She had never believed she would feel this way again, but this was an entirely new spring for her. Desire was exploding inside her; her body was bursting into flower as he touched and caressed her.

Naked above her, Patrick muttered, 'I won't hurt you, darling,' but she wasn't listening to what he said. She was obsessed with a need to stroke his smooth, tanned skin, finger the muscular power of his broad shoulders, deep chest. His body was so different from her own. The hard male force of it fascinated her; she kissed him passionately, mouth open, her tongue tasting the salt of his skin, moving down the rough hair-line on his body.

It wasn't until Patrick parted her thighs and moved between them that she woke up from her own drive for pleasure, and threw a startled, anxious look upwards, stiffening.

The panic came back in a rush and she arched; her muscles flexed, resisting, a scream of fear choking in her throat.

She didn't know him. She didn't recognise his face. He looked so different, darkly flushed, features set and remorseless, harshly male, terrifying. The stranger in the dark was back and Antonia began to fight him off, struggling and gasping with fear.

She was too late to stop him. She felt the force of his body enter her and fought, instinctively using the only weapons she had—digging her nails into his back, her body writhing, heaving, kicking.

'Stop it, Antonia, I thought we were past all that!' Patrick said harshly, lifting his body, his hands gripping her shoulders as he looked down at her.

She couldn't speak, but now that he was lying still and heavy on top of her she stopped fighting and breathed hoarsely, eyes closed, tears trickling down her face.

'I . . . you . . .'

'Am I hurting you?'

She shook her head.

'What did I do that triggerred off that outburst, then?'

'I'm sorry,' she whispered, her hands shifting nervously on his back. She felt the scratches she had inflicted, biting her lip.

'I hurt you,' she wept. 'You're bleeding.'

'It doesn't matter,' Patrick said impatiently.

'It does. I didn't mean to; I'm sorry,' she said, tears still welling up in her eyes. His back was so smooth and powerful. She badly wanted to stroke it again, to let her fingers follow the deep indentation of his spine downwards to the firm buttocks, but she couldn't now; she had spoilt everything.

'Stop crying, Antonia! I can't stand hearing you cry like that; you sound like a sad little girl. I'm sorry, I shouldn't have gone on, but I thought you were ready; I was so sure you wanted it too.'

He moved and she knew he was leaving her; she couldn't bear it. She clung stupidly, both arms round him and felt his body tense, felt the deep intake of his breath.

Roughly he muttered, 'Make up your mind, Antonia. What do you think you're doing to me? I'm only flesh and blood; I can't play these on-off games without losing control sooner or later.' He lifted his head and stared down at her tear-stained, flushed face. 'It's up to you; it always has been. You'll have to say it. Do you want me or don't you?'

'Yes,' she said hoarsely, her legs closing round him too, moving restlessly, invitingly, underneath him, and Patrick began to breathe thickly.

'Well, just don't change your mind again; I won't be responsible if you do.' He bent and lightly kissed her wet eyes, his mouth brushing across her long, damp lashes. 'No more tears, though.'

She sighed. 'If only I could forget that night ever happened!'

He was silent for a second, then he said softly, 'Pretend it didn't, if it helps—tell yourself that that other night was just a nightmare. Tonight is all that matters.'

The words echoed in her head—tonight is all that matters; this is all that matters—and she knew it was true, that the only thing in the world that mattered to her now was his body moving on her, inside her, a tormentingly slow, sensuous intimacy that only began to build in rhythm and power when at last she moved with him, excited past caring if it hurt, arching to meet the deep thrust of his body with a sensation that was way past pleasure, on the borders of ecstasy.

She cried out his name, sobbing it. 'Oh, Patrick...Patrick...' She was boneless, so weak that she was melting into him, surrendering herself to the hard, naked flesh which had become a part of her.

And then, as they moved together towards the climax of their pleasure, a voice called from downstairs. 'Tonia! Where are you? Aren't you dressed yet? Need any help?'

Flushed and breathing wildly, they both froze, their bodies still vibrating.

'Alex!' whispered Antonia, distraught.

Patrick gave a hoarse, frustrated groan. 'I didn't even lock the door!' he muttered through his teeth.

A second later he was on his feet beside the bed. Shivering, Antonia watched his naked body move silently across the room to the door. He locked it, then began dressing in a tearing hurry. Antonia stumbled off the bed just as footsteps sounded on the stairs. A moment later, Alex tried the door, knocked on it, then shouted through it teasingly.

'Tonia? Aren't you ready? We've got a surprise waiting for you downstairs!'

Trying to keep her voice steady, she said, 'Sorry, after my bath I had a short nap on my bed, and I haven't got my dress on yet. I won't take very long; I'll be down in about ten minutes.'

'Need any help? Shall I get Susan-Jane to come up and give you a hand?'

'No, I'll manage.'

'OK. But hurry up; don't forget your surprise is waiting!' Alex laughed and went back downstairs at a run.

Patrick was already fully dressed; he was just tying his tie in front of the mirror; and Antonia couldn't quite meet his eyes as he looked across the room at her.

'How the hell am I going to get out of here without them knowing I was with you?' he asked her.

'I don't know, and God knows what they're all going to think; it's going to be so embarrassing,' she muttered, deeply flushed and feeling light-headed. 'Alex is going to be shocked; I should never have...' She broke off, ran into the bathroom and spent some time washing again, didn't come out for some minutes, and when she did found the bedroom empty.

The door was still locked; Patrick hadn't gone out that way, but the window was open. She went over there just in time to see him drop down on top of the wall. He swayed there, a tall, supple figure in black evening dress, his arms out, as he balanced, like a trapeze artist. He had obviously climbed from her balcony on to the next one, lowered himself from the edge of that, and let himself down that way. Antonia was glad she hadn't been here watching him; her heart would have been in her mouth. It had been a stupid, reckless thing to do. Thank heaven he had landed safely.

She watched him jump down on the other side of the wall, and turned back into the room. There was a hot ache of frustration inside her; she was feverish and chill, the blood beating in her ears. Why had Alex and Susan-Jane come back at that moment? If they had come ten minutes later... five minutes later...

She mustn't think about it. Very flushed, she began to get ready, stepping first into the light, floating black and silver feather dress.

It took her nearly a quarter of an hour in the end. She had to do her make-up and hair again, as well as dress, and her hands were very unsteady. When she was finally ready she paused to assess her reflection in the mirror, her mask firmly in place. The unfamiliar figure gazed back at her, mysterious, ethereal, a creature from another world, as Patrick had said. She didn't recognise herself and it made her feel more confident, more at ease, as she went downstairs. Nobody would be able to read her feelings tonight; she was safe behind her mask.

The party was already under way; there were people in all the ground-floor rooms, and spilling out into the garden. As Antonia appeared heads turned; there was a silence, then a murmur of appreciation. People called out greetings, admiring remarks.

'*Magnifica, cara* . . .'

'Beautiful, darling . . .'

One of Susan-Jane's model friends said sulkily, 'Nobody said this was a fancy-dress party or I'd have worn one too!'

A man asked his wife, 'What is she meant to be? Who is that inside it?'

'She's a bird, stupid!' his wife retorted. 'I think it's Antonia. Is that you, Antonia? You look wonderful.'

She smiled, said thank you, and said the other woman looked gorgeous too, which was true.

'Thanks,' the woman said, complacently smoothing her brief, glittering gold lamé dress with one hand.

'Is it a carnival costume?' asked someone else, and she nodded.

'It must be as light as a feather,' someone else joked, and everyone groaned.

'What an awful joke!'

All the time she kept moving, looking for Alex, wondering if Patrick was with him, if he had come in through the front door as if he had never been here earlier.

She eventually found them in the garden, with glasses of champagne in their hands, by the fountain, which was spraying glittering drops of water into the air.

Patrick was standing facing her; Alex was sitting on the edge of the fountain. They were talking to a man in a dark suit who had his back to her.

As she slowly drifted towards them, her long feather skirts floating around her, Alex caught sight of her and waved, his face lighting up in a smile. 'There you are at last, Antonia! You look quite wonderful.'

She smiled back, glad of her mask, very conscious of Patrick's dark, unsmiling glance, taken aback by the grimness of his expression. Why was he looking at her like that, as if he hated her?

Then the man in the dark suit turned, smiling, holding out his hands. 'Hallo, darling! Surprise, surprise!'

It was Cy.

# CHAPTER EIGHT

SOMEHOW Antonia went on walking towards them, even more relieved to be wearing the mask of feathers, which could hide her expression, her feelings, what she was thinking. Shyly, she put her hands into Cy's, and he bent and kissed her lightly on the cheek, laughing as he straightened.

'Your feathers tickle!' Cy said, laughing, and then moving back a step to contemplate her. 'I remember you wore that at Patsy's ball and it made a sensation. It suits you; there has always been something bird-like about you. You look enchanting in it.'

Out of the corner of her eye she saw Patrick's face stiffen, his mouth a white, angry line.

Neither Cy nor Alex noticed his expression; they weren't looking at him, either directly or secretly, like Antonia. Alex was smiling indulgently at her. Without even glancing at Patrick, Alex said, 'Come on, Patrick, let's go back inside and see how the party's going on, and leave the love-birds to bill and coo out here alone.'

Antonia flinched at that and felt Patrick watching her, his face hostile, picking up the vibration of her reaction, his eyes coldly probing to work out what she felt.

'See you later, Cy,' Alex said, grinning at him. 'Don't expect to have the garden to yourself for much longer, though. I warn you, people always come out here to dance, so if you want to kiss the girl properly get on with it before you get interrupted! I'll keep them inside for as long as I can, but I can't promise anything!'

Patrick grimly strode away towards the house, his lean, dark figure tense as a drawn sword. She quivered as he passed her, her nerves jumping, but he didn't look in her direction, and was gone a second later, followed at once by Alex.

She sank down nervelessly on the bench under the fig tree and Cy came and sat beside her, taking her hand, stroking her fingers gently.

'Glad to see me, Antonia?'

She stared up at him, finding his face oddly unfamiliar, remote. He wasn't far off forty, a tall, spare, austere man with dusty-coloured hair slipping back off his forehead, dark eyes and a thin, pale face. Work occupied most of his time; although he was wealthy he took even his pleasures seriously, but then Cy was a serious man with a strong sense of responsibility and duty. That was why Antonia had felt safe whenever she was with him.

She didn't feel safe now. She felt as if she were walking a slippery edge over a cliff fall. She wished Cy had not come back to Venice now.

'I'm always glad to see you, Cy,' she lied, huskily, and he smiled at her.

'I was very concerned after we talked last night, Tonia. Thinking over what you had said, I realised it was vital that we talked, face to face, so I moved heaven and earth to rearrange my appointments for today and tomorrow, flew down to New York from Boston, managed to get a seat on Concorde at the very last minute, arrived in London at midnight last night...'

'You can't have got there that soon! We only talked at around nine o'clock that evening.'

'You're forgetting the time difference.' He smiled indulgently. 'It was nine in the evening for you, but mid-afternoon for me. I booked into an airport hotel, and slept quite late, because I knew I'd have to wait until the afternoon for a seat on a plane to Venice. I flew in three hours ago.'

'You must be exhausted! You shouldn't have rushed all this way just to see me! If I'd known you were thinking of doing this I'd have told you not to!'

'I suspected as much; that's why I didn't warn anyone I was coming.'

'Not even Patsy? I wondered. I saw her this morning and she didn't say a word about you coming.'

'She had no idea. She was amazed when I arrived.'

'So you have been to the *palazzo*? Pasty must have been overjoyed to see you.'

He smiled again, his eyes warm, as they always were when he talked about his aunt.

'Yes, she was as welcoming as ever. I went to the *palazzo* straight from the airport, expecting to find you there, and Patsy told me you were having this party tonight and were helping your uncle and aunt organise everything, and wouldn't be working today, so I didn't come straight round to see you. I talked to Patsy for a while and had a peaceful hour in my room, bathed, changed, then rang your uncle, who promptly invited me to the party. I told him not to tell you I was coming; I wanted to surprise you.'

'You did,' she said, her smile quivering. 'You shouldn't have come all this way, Cy. I was going to write to you, explain...'

He gave a wry little smile. 'That was what I didn't want you to do. I don't think letters are ever very satisfactory. I wanted to talk to you face to face.'

She sighed. 'It would have been much easier for both of us, though, if you had let me explain in a letter. I find it hard to talk about, Cy.'

'I realise that; that's why I've been so careful all these months not to talk about what happened to you. I realised you weren't over it yet, and might not be for a long time. You mustn't be afraid I'm getting impatient, Antonia.'

'It isn't that!' she burst out. 'I mean, that isn't why, not really. It's just that I've realised that...' She stopped, biting her lip, then plunged on, 'That although I like you, I don't love you, Cy, not... not that way... not enough for marriage, and it wouldn't be fair for me to marry you when I know I never could.'

His face had changed while she was speaking, his pale brows meeting. 'I'm not asking you to fall in love with me,' he said with a touch of impatience, even irritation. 'I thought you understood that. I'm not a romantic teenager, looking for the girl of my dreams; I'm not going to expect too much from you and I hoped you wouldn't expect too much from me. I thought we suited each other. I'm fond of you; I like you very much. You fit in with my lifestyle, with Patsy, with the *palazzo*. I think you would be a comfortable wife, in spite of the fact that you're so much younger. As I'm so much older than you, that could have been a problem, but in your case I felt it was an asset.'

She gazed at him dumbly through her mask. He had never talked like this before. As what he had said sank in, she realised that she had made false assumptions about Cy.

'After your experience two years ago I realised you had been put off sex, maybe for life,' he coolly went on. 'That was partly why I proposed in the first place.'

Antonia's mouth parted on a silent gasp, but her feather mask hid from Cy her look of incredulity.

He shrugged casually. 'Frankly, I've never been highly sexed, myself; I suppose that's why I haven't married yet. I like women's company, but I've always been too busy to look for a wife. But I'll be forty soon, Patsy kept telling me to get married, and she thought you would be an ideal wife for me. She likes you; she felt you would fit in.'

It had never entered Antonia's head that Patsy might have engineered her engagement. She felt a fool. She had even wondered if Patsy might resent her!

'That was why I stayed on at the *palazzo* this summer—to get to know you,' said Cy quietly. 'I thought at first that Pasty was crazy, you were far too young— but Patsy pointed out that that made it easier for us to guide you, help you learn to run the *palazzo*, learn to fit into our lifestyle. I felt I could trust you not to cheat on me with other men, or embarrass me. I thought you would be happy with what I could offer you, the sort of life we would have together. I'm a man of set habits and a liking for a quiet life who only wants someone to share my life with, someone suitable. So if you are afraid I'll be disappointed because you can't offer me wild passion, you needn't be. Sex seems to me to be a rather overrated part of life. I admit, I'd like a child—that's my main reason for wanting to marry, in fact—but we needn't rush it. There is plenty of time for that.'

Antonia couldn't think how to answer him. Although he had never been quite so blunt about why he had proposed to her, he had been fairly honest, she had to admit. He had never claimed to be in love with her, had never tried to do more than kiss her lightly. She had told herself he was sensitive, caring. Now she realised he was totally indifferent to her, sexually.

He hadn't tried to make love to her because he hadn't wanted her! She was stunned as it dawned on her what her life would have been like if she'd married him. She had been so self-obsessed that she hadn't actually listened to what Cy had told her in the past. She had heard without understanding, but now it was all very clear. Terribly clear.

Cy had actually chosen her because she was so withdrawn and emotionally muted. He wanted someone he could manipulate into becoming the sort of show wife he wanted—someone to run his homes, someone who knew all about art and antiques, could be trusted to look after the Devvon collections, someone who was well brought up and could be shown off to his friends, colleagues and clients, someone who was young enough to be totally obedient.

Even the fact that she had been scarred by that attack on the beach had made her a suitable wife for Cy, because it meant she wouldn't make any emotional demands on him. She would never expect Cy to love her with any depth or real feeling. She wouldn't want what Cy couldn't give her.

He hadn't wanted a real woman of flesh and blood at all. She had been worried about telling him she didn't want to marry him after all; she had hated the idea of hurting his feelings. The irony of that stunned her. She couldn't make him unhappy. Cy had never had any feelings for her except a vague kindness and distant affection. He would have made her unutterably miserable once she'd realised what a mistake she had made.

Quietly, she said, 'I'm sorry, Cy. We both made a mistake, I'm afraid. I don't think I would make the sort of wife you want.' She slowly pulled off her ring and held it out.

Cy opened his hand and she dropped it into his palm. He stared down at the glittering diamond. 'You haven't explained why! Don't you think you owe me some sort of explanation? What made you change your mind?'

She sighed. 'It's too complicated to explain. I changed my mind, that's all. Please don't make it hard, Cy. I do know what I'm doing. I'll give up my job at the *palazzo* at once, and move out. I'm sure Patsy will have no trouble finding someone else to do it. Maybe the next girl will be more suitable for you than I am.'

Cy reddened. 'That's insulting; I don't think I deserve that!'

She bit her lip. 'I'm sorry, I didn't mean to insult you,' she said quietly. 'All I meant was that I hoped you'd find someone else. I'm sure you will if you want to; the world must be full of girls who would give their eye-teeth for what you're offering. You have a lot to offer, I know that—you're a kind man, and a generous one; any woman who married you would have a marvellous lifestyle, and Patsy is a darling. Someone else will grab you with both hands. It's just that I finally realised I wanted something else. I like you, too, Cy, and I'm fond of you, but for me that isn't enough.'

He stood up abruptly, walked over to the fountain, and put a hand into the flying spray, his back to Antonia.

'Patsy will be very disappointed—she was very happy over our engagement—but I think you should talk to her before you make any decision about giving up your job. She's very pleased with the way you've been dealing with the cataloguing. I don't think she'll want to lose you. I shall fly back almost at once, so you needn't be afraid of running into me at the *palazzo*. I suggest you stay on at least while Patsy is in Venice.'

Antonia didn't know how to answer that. If Patsy was angry it would be impossible for her to stay, but she said at last, 'I'll talk to her tomorrow.'

'Good,' said Cy, turning back to face her, his cool mask back in place. 'It would cause too much talk if I left the party straight away. We had better go back into the house and mingle with the other guests.' He held out his hand with the ring still on the palm. 'Please wear this just for tonight, Antonia. You can leave it at the *palazzo* tomorrow, but it would be embarrassing if someone here noticed you weren't wearing it. It would require explanations and that would be tiresome.'

Her instinct was to refuse, but then she looked into his eyes and saw that he was afraid of more than embarrassment; Cy was a very formal man, with a strong sense of his own dignity and status, and he was afraid of being humiliated publicly, of everyone knowing that she had broken off their engagement, especially after he had flown all this way to see her.

Reluctantly she took the ring and slid it back on to her finger, repressing an instinctive shudder as she felt the cold metal closing round her flesh again.

Taking it off and giving it back to him had made her feel free; now she was trapped again.

'Can I also ask you not to tell anyone our engagement is off until I've left for New York?' Cy flatly asked, and she nodded.

'I won't.'

'Not even your aunt and uncle?' Cy insisted.

'I won't tell anyone,' she promised, and he gave a short sigh.

'Thank you.'

The rest of the evening was a blur to Antonia. She and Cy went back into the little pink house, which by now was crammed with people talking, laughing, drinking and eating, the sound of their chatter even drowning the music playing on the stereo system. Cy got her a drink and started talking to a friend of Patsy Devvon; Antonia briefly stayed with them, then drifted off discreetly and found herself a spot in a corner, sipped her drink, nibbled party food, pretending to listen to one of Alex's friends, smiling, trying to look happy, while all the time she was dying to get out of there, away from all these people, away from Cy and Patrick and the crazy confusion of her life.

People moved out into the garden later and Susan-Jane turned the stereo up, so that they could hear the tape of the latest pop music out there. People began dancing.

After a while Alex came back into the house. 'I want to waltz,' he said. 'Let's be old-fashioned and romantic, shall we? It is our last evening here.' He changed the tape to one of swirling Strauss waltzes and drew Susan-Jane out into the garden, where some of the guests were laughingly making disgusted noises over the change of music.

'We can't dance to this!' said a teenage daughter of one of Susan-Jane's friends.

'People have for years. Watch us! We'll show you how!' Alex said defiantly, beginning to dance with his wife.

Cy turned and looked at Antonia, walked over to her corner. 'I can at least waltz. Let's have one dance, then I'm going,' he said coolly, taking her hand.

As they walked out into the garden she saw Patrick with a group by the fig tree. His blue eyes narrowed, hard as cold slate, watching them as Cy put an arm around her waist and drew her into his arms. He danced well but Antonia felt clumsy, stumbling, very aware of those angry, hostile eyes watching them.

The waltz seemed to go on forever. She was dying for the music to stop; she ached to escape. She couldn't bear Patrick watching her with those enemy eyes.

At last the tape ended and everyone clamoured to have some modern music back. Laughing, Alex capitulated. Cy released Antonia, looked at his watch, and made a big thing of yawning.

'I've got jet-lag, a very bad headache,' he said. 'I think I should be going. Are you coming back to the *palazzo*, or will you stay for the rest of the party?'

Susan-Jane overheard the question and came over to them, putting an arm around Antonia. 'Oh, don't go yet, darling. We won't see you again for ages. Stay on for the rest of the party; you can see Cy tomorrow, after all!'

Cy nodded, and smiled at Susan-Jane. 'Of course she can. Yes, do stay on, Antonia. I'll see you tomorrow morning at breakfast, then.' He made a few polite remarks to Alex and his wife. 'Have a safe journey to Monte Carlo; I'm sure we'll be meeting again very soon.'

'No wedding date set yet?' asked Alex blithely, and Antonia stiffened, her face pale under the feather mask, conscious of Cy's well-disguised embarrassment.

'We're talking about it,' Cy said coolly, and she had to admire his ability to hide his true feelings.

He bent, and lightly kissed Antonia's cheek. 'Enjoy your party,' he said and walked away through the noisy throng. Antonia stared after him, feeling odd. Had she ever really believed she would marry him? She found it hard to remember. Cy had come into her life and was going out again as suddenly, leaving almost no real impression on her. He was as unreal as the *palazzo* he would one day inherit—priceless, mysterious, remote. She had never felt at home there. She was sure she never would have done.

'Missing him already?' Susan-Jane asked, watching her wistful face. 'Do you want to change your mind and run after him? He did come all this way to see you; maybe we shouldn't be so selfish, asking you to stay.'

Antonia turned, shaking her head. 'He's very tired—he's got jet-lag. He just wants to sleep for hours; there's no point in going with him anyway.'

'How long is he going to stay in Venice?' asked Alex, and behind him she saw Patrick loom up, dark as a winter storm, his face rigid.

Confused, she stammered, 'I d... don't know; not l... long...'

'Maybe he wants you to go back to the States with him?' Alex suggested. 'Being so far apart isn't much fun for an engaged couple! Or does he want to get married sooner?'

Patrick watched her, his eyes icy with a cruelty that made her wince.

'No, it isn't that,' she said helplessly, trying to think of some excuse they would accept. 'H . . . he came to see Patsy, not me, to talk about important family business.' The lie made her blush, but she hoped they wouldn't see that under her mask.

'Oh, is that it?' Alex asked, making a face. 'Well, if you will marry an accountant, darling, that's what you get!'

One of his friends, a Venice restaurateur, came up at that moment and smiled at Antonia. 'Dance with me, little bird?'

She was grateful for the escape route and thankfully smiled back, nodding. 'Love to, Giorgio.'

He was in his fifties, plump, cheerful and married with six children, but was a notorious flirt. His wife indulgently watched them; she knew Giorgio's flirting meant nothing, and so did Antonia, who laughed at everything he said in her ear.

'I mean it; you're the loveliest girl here,' he said reproachfully, and she grinned up at him.

'How many times have you said that this evening?'

'Girls are so suspicious these days! When I was young girls believed everything a man said to them,' he sighed nostalgically.

'I bet they didn't! They just let you think they did!'

They were dancing in the garden under fairy-lights rigged up by Alex. The silken lining of her dress made it slide smoothly against her skin, the black and silver feathers glittered in the coloured lights, and people kept looking at her with fascination. It should have been romantic, glamorous, exciting. But Antonia had to work hard to keep smiling; her heart was as heavy as lead inside her.

She was intensely aware of Patrick on the other side of the garden, watching her dance with Giorgio, his icy blue eyes missing nothing. He hadn't danced with anyone. He wasn't talking to anyone. He just leaned against the fig tree, arms folded, his body tense, never moving his eyes from her, and his expression made her shiver.

One of the older generation began clamouring for more waltzing, and Alex put that tape back on, to the disgust of the younger people.

Giorgio smiled down at her happily. 'This is better!'

She wasn't so sure, but smiled back politely, then her heart gave a wild leap as Patrick loomed up behind them and tapped Giorgio on the shoulder.

'Mind if I steal your partner?' he curtly asked.

Giorgio looked round, began, 'Yes, I do...' then met Patrick's dangerous stare and stopped speaking, looked alarmed, moved instinctively away from her, dropping her hand.

'Is that OK with you, Antonia?' he asked, though, as if having his doubts about leaving her alone with a man who looked like Patrick.

Patrick's eyes burnt into her, silently compelling her to agree.

She swallowed, nodded, speechless.

She wanted to turn and run, but with all those people around how could she, without making a scene? Patrick slid a hand around her waist. She quivered in response to his touch, and her treacherous body responded by swaying close to him, irresistibly drawn to what it wanted.

They began to dance, her head level with his shoulder; she was bitterly tempted to shut her eyes and let her head fall against him, but she couldn't do that, so she gazed fixedly over his shoulder instead, her feet stumbling.

'Sorry,' she mumbled, and he stopped, looked down at her with those hard, angry eyes.

'You're still going to marry him, aren't you?' he bit out, and she felt people glancing at them, startled by his expression, even if they couldn't quite hear what he was saying. 'In spite of everything, you're still going through with it?'

She broke away from him, afraid of what he might say or do next, and ran into the house. People looked round at her as she fled past, her feathered skirts brushing against them, floating around her. Patrick was on her heels. Some people began laughing, thinking it was some sort of game, a party joke; they couldn't see her face under her mask and Patrick had masked his expression, too.

She made for the stairs, thinking, He won't dare follow me up there! She heard Alex stop him, saying in a puzzled voice, 'What's going on, Patrick?' and felt able to slow down a little, her breathing rapid and her heart thudding against her ribs.

If she imagined Alex would keep him there she soon realised she was wrong. She didn't catch what he said to Alex, but he was soon coming after her again, taking the stairs two at a time. Despairingly, Antonia raced towards the door of her old room.

She got it open, ran through, turned to slam the door shut and bolt it, but Patrick hurled himself against the panels from some feet away. The door crashed open again, sending her flying. She and Patrick landed in a huddle together on the floor.

The thud they made must have been heard downstairs; the ceiling must have shaken; the old Venetian glass lampshades must have dipped and swayed, tinkling like bells. Everyone downstairs had hushed, the voices faded; they must be staring upwards, mouths open.

What on earth would they be thinking?

She struggled to sit up, flushed and distraught, discovered that some of the feathers on her dress were broken, snapped off by the fall, and it seemed the last straw. She snapped too, furiously shouted at Patrick.

'Look what you've done! My lovely dress... ruined... and what do you think everyone at the party is thinking? They'll be talking nineteen to the dozen downstairs... This will be all round Venice tomorrow!'

'Damn them; damn Venice,' said Patrick through his teeth. 'What do any of them matter?'

'I don't want to be gossiped about all over the city!' she half sobbed, picking up feathers from all over the floor.

A sound at the door made them both look round. Alex stood there, framed in the doorway, his face alert.

'Moulting, Antonia?' he asked her, then before she could answer said more seriously, 'What exactly is going on?'

'Keep out of this, Alex,' Patrick said brusquely.

For once Alex's friendly tolerance was missing. He scowled at Patrick. 'She's my niece, guy. And this is my house—for tonight, at least. That makes this my business. Antonia, is he bothering you? Shall I kick him out?'

Patrick turned his head and looked down into her eyes, silent, yet wordlessly compelling her.

She bit her lips, looked down, shook her head.

'What does that mean?' asked Alex. 'What the hell is all this, anyway?'

'She's an adult, Alex, not a child,' Patrick said. 'And this is a private discussion. Will you please go back to your party?'

Alex still lingered, frowning uncertainly, watching her. 'Antonia?' he asked one more time.

'I'll be OK,' she whispered, not meeting his eyes.

'Well, if you need me, yell,' Alex said slowly, then she heard the door shut, his footsteps on the stairs.

There was a silence, then Patrick said, 'As I was saying when your uncle arrived, you can't marry that guy. Now I've met him I can't believe you ever said you would. I know you say he makes you feel safe, but it will be the safety of a gaol, Antonia. Oh, it will be a luxurious cell, and no doubt he's kind and generous, but he's also a good fifteen years older than you, he's almost bald now, and he's boring, Antonia. Don't pretend you don't think so. I saw your face when you were with him. He bores you. You went into this engagement like a sleep-walker, not really aware what you were doing, but any day now you're going to wake up and realise you're trapped, and by then it could be too late to get away.'

She had promised Cy she wouldn't tell anyone that their engagement was over. She turned away, her face pale and mutinous, troubled.

'I don't want to talk about it,' she said.

'Of course you don't! Reality might break in, and you can't take too much reality, can you, Antonia?' Contempt grated in his voice and she flinched.

'Oh, go away, leave me alone! Alex...everyone downstairs...will be wondering what we're doing up here.'

Patrick's eyes gleamed, a vivid, electrifying blue. 'You mean they'll wonder if we're making love?'

'No!' she contradicted, a rush of hot blood entering her face.

'Of course they will!' he muttered. A pause, then he said huskily, 'And I've thought about nothing else all evening.'

Everything in her stopped: her heart stopped beating; her mind stopped working; her lungs stopped drawing in air. For a beat of time she just looked at him, suspended in space; and the sound of his husky voice was like the oceanic roar of her own blood as she heard it begin pumping again. Everything inside her began again. She was reborn. The shock of rebirth made her shake violently, barely able to stand.

'Oh, Patrick,' she whispered, looking at his mouth, aching for the touch of it.

His facial bones were tightly clenched, his darkly flushed skin taut over them. 'I've been dying of frustration ever since Alex and his wife interrupted us,' he said in a deep, hoarse voice. 'I need you, Antonia.'

Helplessly she swayed towards him, captive to the sound of his voice, forgetting everything else in her own driving need for completion. She had been aching with frustration too, all evening.

Patrick put his head down and she felt him kissing her throat, burying his mouth in her, his lips apart, the moist heat of his mouth sending shudders down her back. His arm closed possessively round her, pulling her so close that their bodies almost merged. 'You can't marry

Cy Devvon,' he muttered. 'I couldn't bear it if you did, Antonia. You've got to marry me, not him. Don't you know I'm desperately in love with you?'

Her heart turned over and over like a bird in ecstatic flight, skimming and soaring on spiral winds.

She gazed up at him through the eye-holes of her mask, trembling convulsively as what he had said sank in... He loved her; he wanted to marry her. She had known he wanted her, desired her; but until now she had been afraid to hope that he actually loved her.

He watched her face as if waiting for some answer, groaned impatiently. 'I want to see what's going on inside that head of yours! Take that damned mask off!' He reached behind her, fumbled with the strings; the mask fell down and fluttered to the floor beside them, but Antonia didn't even notice.

All she could see was Patrick's hard, insistent face, the deep blue eyes hunting over her features.

'Tell me the truth—how do you really feel about me, Antonia?' he asked in that tense, shaken voice, and she gave a long sigh.

'I love you,' she whispered and heard his sharp intake of breath.

He caught her face between his hands. 'Darling,' he said thickly, kissing her with fire and compulsion. Her head began to spin; she wound her arms around his neck and kissed him back with a hunger that made Patrick tremble, muttering her name into her yielding mouth.

Antonia fell into that soft velvety darkness again, her eyes shut, her whole body given up to his hands, her mouth quivering wildly under his. The dreams which had haunted her for two years had become her reality. Past and present merged; her blood ran hotly with desire.

Patrick broke off the long kiss at last, groaning, 'What I want to do is take you to bed, but I'm afraid that any minute now Alex is coming back, and we can't just lock the door and to hell with him; he would think I was murdering you, and break the door down.'

She laughed unsteadily, leaning on him. 'Poor Alex; he must be feeling very worried.'

'Not as worried as I was when your fiancé arrived!' Patrick said grimly, looking into her eyes. 'One minute I was so sure you were mine—we'd been making love so passionately before the party—and the next he walked in and when I saw the two of you together I was terrified you were going to go through with that marriage.'

She hesitated, torn between her promise to Cy and her need to tell Patrick the truth.

'No, I wouldn't have,' she finally compromised.

Patrick searched her face, grimacing. 'Well, I wasn't so sure. I knew he could offer you a lot more than I could, materially. He's rich and that *palazzo* of his would be a big temptation to anyone; and you had said he made you feel safe. I was afraid you'd opt for safety and security.'

'No, I'm opting for love,' she said softly, and saw his mouth curve into a smile.

He took her hand, looked at the ring glittering on it, and made a wry face. 'Take this off, Antonia; I can't bear to see it on your finger.'

'Not yet, not tonight, Patrick,' she said and saw his face tighten, his eyes lift to look at her angrily. She had given Cy that promise, yet she couldn't let Patrick think she was undecided. She had to explain. 'Promise me you won't tell anyone else yet,' she pleaded. 'But...well...I've already told Cy that I won't marry him...'

That shook him. His eyes narrowed, startled. 'You have? Why didn't you tell me earlier? Why let me think you might go on with it? You put me through torture.'

'I'm sorry, Patrick, I didn't want to...but, you see, I promised Cy I wouldn't tell anyone until he had left Venice again. He's going immediately. But he asked me to keep my ring on until he had gone, then put it in the safe at the *palazzo*. He didn't want anyone here to know yet, and I felt I had to agree. Cy has a strong sense of his own dignity, his status here in Venice. He's such a serious man; he hates being embarrassed, and hates even more the idea of losing face. He wanted to get back to Boston, where nobody knew me. I expect he'll tell all his friends there that it was he who broke the engagement.'

Patrick watched her with shrewd, thoughtful eyes. 'You don't say you're afraid you've hurt him badly, I notice. He didn't really love you, did he?'

She shook her head, smiled at him wryly. 'No, you're right. He never did.'

'I suspected it right from the beginning, although I didn't know the guy, and could only guess,' Patrick said. 'He'd got engaged to you then flown back to the States and left you here. I worked out that that could mean one of two things. Either he was crazy about you and was afraid to stampede you in case he panicked you and you ran away from him, so had gone back to New York to let you get used to the idea of marrying him—that was a possibility, and would mean he was a very shrewd guy with the confidence to risk leaving you here alone— or, on the other hand, he was a cold fish who wasn't in love with you at all.'

'Cy isn't so much cold as cool, but you're right. He wasn't in love with me. He just decided it was time he got married, and I was there at the right time, and seemed a suitable choice. He was very frank about that tonight. I hadn't realised what he was really like or what he really wanted from me.' She broke off and sighed. 'Well, it doesn't seem fair to him to talk about that. He didn't hurt me, and I didn't hurt him. That's all that matters.'

Patrick nodded. 'You're right. It's easy to hurt other people without meaning to. I'm glad you didn't have to hurt him.'

Antonia watched his face uncertainly. 'Patrick, we've never talked about... about Laura... Don't you think we should?'

He gave a short sigh, shrugged. 'You know everything important, Antonia. I was in love with her, and we were going to be married, and then she met someone else and fell in love with him. At the time I was very bitter, but since I met you I've realised what happened to her, because it has happened to me now.'

Happiness flooded through her; her eyes shone like the sea on a summer day, and Patrick smiled down at her passionately.

'Laura got engaged to me because I asked her and there wasn't anybody else in her life then. But I was just someone she liked and was fond of—she was never in love with me—and when she met a man who really turned her on she realised she'd made a mistake. If she had married me we would both have been unhappy once I realised she was never going to love me the way I did her.'

Antonia caught her breath, jealousy and pain stabbing her, and Patrick looked down at her, searching her expression.

'Darling, don't look like that.' He kissed her softly, stroking her cheek with one long index finger. 'Don't you see? I got over Laura long ago. She doesn't matter a damn to me now; I've accepted she made the right decision. In fact, ever since I met you again, found myself falling in love with you, I've been grateful to her. I love you far more than I ever loved Laura.'

'But that night...in Bordighera...you only looked at me because you thought I was like her,' Antonia whispered.

'That was why I first stared at you,' he admitted. 'But then I saw you didn't look like her, and I still found myself attracted... When the police accused me of attacking you I was confused enough not even to be sure I wasn't guilty, because I knew I'd wanted you while I was looking at you at that party. In fact, that was why I was so angry at the time. I was furious with myself for wanting you that way, especially after I heard what had happened. I almost felt it had been me——'

She was pale, shaken. 'Patrick! And I used to dream...' She stopped, biting her lip, and he stared, frowning.

'Dream?' He watched her shrewdly, then slowly said, 'That it had been me?'

She nodded silently, seeing the shock and anger in his face, and frightened of his reaction.

'So that was why you were so terrified when you met me again? Why you were scared to admit you wanted me to make love to you?' he said harshly.

Afraid of his rage, she clung to him, burying her face in his chest, mumbling into his shirt. 'Don't look so hurt! Don't be angry with me!'

He held her, kissed her hair, his voice rough. 'I'm not angry with you, darling. If I'm angry it isn't with you, it's because of what happened to you.'

'I felt it was my fault,' she confessed at last, her face hidden against his shirt, hearing the strong beat of his heart very close to her, and reassured by the rhythm and strength of it. 'I wanted you that night; I fell in love with you at first sight and I had to follow you down to that beach, and that's why... why... it happened.'

'Oh, my God, is that what you've been thinking all this time? I knew there was something you were holding back, that it wasn't just the obvious fear; I sensed something else was upsetting you,' Patrick ground out. 'You've been blaming yourself for what that swine did to you. How could you believe that anyone would think it was your fault?'

'I thought it was!' she said with a little muffled sound, half sob, half anguished laughter. 'I know my parents would have been shocked if they'd known I had followed you down to that beach because I was so attracted to you. They'd have said I was asking for what happened.'

His brows met angrily. 'In this day and age? I'm sure they wouldn't, Antonia.'

'But it's true, in a way. If I hadn't followed you it wouldn't have happened—you can't deny that—and you had made it crystal-clear that you weren't interested in me! You gave me that brush-off.'

He groaned. 'Darling...'

She smiled at him quiveringly. 'No, it wasn't your fault. You were unhappy over Laura. I understood that later. But ever since I've had such strange dreams; it was all so mixed up in my head—my feelings about you, about what had happened. It was as if I'd been punished for feeling that way about you. I was left scarred, afraid to feel anything for any man after that, in case I got punished again.'

His face was sombre. 'And now? How do you feel now?' he asked quietly, his voice very deep, tipping her head back with a gentle hand so that he could see her face more clearly.

Antonia looked into his commanding blue eyes and a wave of intense feeling went through her.

'I feel...' She paused, hunting for the right word. 'Free...' she whispered at last. 'I love you so much, Patrick.'

He took her into his arms and kissed her passionately. Antonia kissed him back, happier than she had ever been in her life before. She knew she would never quite be able to forget that dark night in Bordighera, but Patrick's love had healed the wounds of terror and passion. He had been her first love, and he would be her first lover; together they would lay the ghosts that had haunted her for two years.

# IT'S FREE! IT'S FUN! ENTER THE

☆ "Hooray for ☆
☆ Hollywood" ☆
## SWEEPSTAKES!

**W**e're giving away prizes to celebrate the screening of four new romance movies on CBS TV this fall! Look for the movies on four Sunday afternoons in October. And be sure to return your Official Entry Coupons to try for a fabulous vacation in Hollywood!

⭐ If you're the Grand Prize winner we'll fly you and your companion to Los Angeles for a 7-day/6-night vacation you'll never forget!

⭐ You'll stay at the luxurious Regent Beverly Wilshire Hotel,* a prime location for celebrity spotting!

⭐ You'll have time to visit Universal Studios,* stroll the Hollywood Walk of Fame, check out celebrities' footprints at Mann's Chinese Theater, ride a trolley to see the homes of the stars, and more!

⭐ The prize includes a rental car for 7 days and $1,000.00 pocket money!

**Someone's going to win this fabulous prize, and it might just be you! Remember, the more times you enter, the better your chances of winning!**

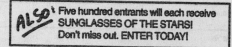

ALSO* Five hundred entrants will each receive SUNGLASSES OF THE STARS! Don't miss out. ENTER TODAY!

The proprietors of the trademark are not associated with this promotion.

CBSIBC

# Take 4 bestselling love stories FREE

## Plus get a FREE surprise gift!

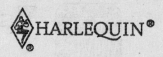

# EDGE OF ETERNITY
## Jasmine Cresswell

Two years after their divorce, David Powell
and Eve Graham met again in Eternity,
Massachusetts—and this time there was magic
between them. But David was tied up in a
murder that no amount of small-town gossip
could free him from. When Eve was pulled into
the frenzy, he knew he had to come up with
some answers—including how to convince her
they should marry again...this time for keeps.

**EDGE OF ETERNITY,** available in
November from Intrigue, is the sixth book in
Harlequin's exciting new cross-line series,
**WEDDINGS, INC.**

Be sure to look for the final book, **VOWS,** by
Margaret Moore (Harlequin Historical #248),
coming in December.

WED6

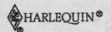  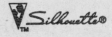

# "HOORAY FOR HOLLYWOOD" SWEEPSTAKES

## HERE'S HOW THE SWEEPSTAKES WORKS

### OFFICIAL RULES — NO PURCHASE NECESSARY

To enter, complete an Official Entry Form or hand print on a 3" x 5" card the words "HOORAY FOR HOLLYWOOD", your name and address and mail your entry in the pre-addressed envelope (if provided) or to: "Hooray for Hollywood" Sweepstakes, P.O. Box 9076, Buffalo, NY 14269-9076 or "Hooray for Hollywood" Sweepstakes, P.O. Box 637, Fort Erie, Ontario L2A 5X3. Entries must be sent via First Class Mail and be received no later than 12/31/94. No liability is assumed for lost, late or misdirected mail.

Winners will be selected in random drawings to be conducted no later than January 31, 1995 from all eligible entries received.

Grand Prize: A 7-day/6-night trip for 2 to Los Angeles, CA including round trip air transportation from commercial airport nearest winner's residence, accommodations at the Regent Beverly Wilshire Hotel, free rental car, and $1,000 spending money. (Approximate prize value which will vary dependent upon winner's residence: $5,400.00 U.S.); 500 Second Prizes: A pair of "Hollywood Star" sunglasses (prize value: $9.95 U.S. each). Winner selection is under the supervision of D.L. Blair, Inc., an independent judging organization, whose decisions are final. Grand Prize travelers must sign and return a release of liability prior to traveling. Trip must be taken by 2/1/96 and is subject to airline schedules and accommodations availability.

Sweepstakes offer is open to residents of the U.S. (except Puerto Rico) and Canada who are 18 years of age or older, except employees and immediate family members of Harlequin Enterprises, Ltd., its affiliates, subsidiaries, and all agencies, entities or persons connected with the use, marketing or conduct of this sweepstakes. All federal, state, provincial, municipal and local laws apply. Offer void wherever prohibited by law. Taxes and/or duties are the sole responsibility of the winners. Any litigation within the province of Quebec respecting the conduct and awarding of prizes may be submitted to the Regie des loteries et courses du Quebec. All prizes will be awarded; winners will be notified by mail. No substitution of prizes are permitted. Odds of winning are dependent upon the number of eligible entries received.

Potential grand prize winner must sign and return an Affidavit of Eligibility within 30 days of notification. In the event of non-compliance within this time period, prize may be awarded to an alternate winner. Prize notification returned as undeliverable may result in the awarding of prize to an alternate winner. By acceptance of their prize, winners consent to use of their names, photographs, or likenesses for purpose of advertising, trade and promotion on behalf of Harlequin Enterprises, Ltd., without further compensation unless prohibited by law. A Canadian winner must correctly answer an arithmetical skill-testing question in order to be awarded the prize.

For a list of winners (available after 2/28/95), send a separate stamped, self-addressed envelope to: Hooray for Hollywood Sweepstakes 3252 Winners, P.O. Box 4200, Blair, NE 68009.

CBSRLS

◉◉◉ **OFFICIAL ENTRY COUPON** ◉◉◉

# "Hooray for Hollywood"
## SWEEPSTAKES!

Yes, I'd love to win the Grand Prize — a vacation in Hollywood — or one of 500 pairs of "sunglasses of the stars"! Please enter me in the sweepstakes!

This entry must be received by December 31, 1994.
Winners will be notified by January 31, 1995.

Name _____

Address _____ Apt. _____

City _____

State/Prov. _____ Zip/Postal Code _____

Daytime phone number _____
(area code)

Mail all entries to: Hooray for Hollywood Sweepstakes,
P.O. Box 9076, Buffalo, NY 14269-9076.
In Canada, mail to: Hooray for Hollywood Sweepstakes,
P.O. Box 637, Fort Erie, ON L2A 5X3.

KCH

---

◉◉◉ **OFFICIAL ENTRY COUPON** ◉◉◉

# "Hooray for Hollywood"
## SWEEPSTAKES!

Yes, I'd love to win the Grand Prize — a vacation in Hollywood — or one of 500 pairs of "sunglasses of the stars"! Please enter me in the sweepstakes!

This entry must be received by December 31, 1994.
Winners will be notified by January 31, 1995.

Name _____

Address _____ Apt. _____

City _____

State/Prov. _____ Zip/Postal Code _____

Daytime phone number _____
(area code)

Mail all entries to: Hooray for Hollywood Sweepstakes,
P.O. Box 9076, Buffalo, NY 14269-9076.
In Canada, mail to: Hooray for Hollywood Sweepstakes,
P.O. Box 637, Fort Erie, ON L2A 5X3.

KCH